FROM 3 TO 26.2

From 3 to 26.2

How I Completed My First Marathon

Stephanie Turner

Order this book online at www.trafford.com
or email orders@trafford.com

Most Trafford titles are also available at major online book retailers.

© Copyright 2010 Stephanie Turner.
All rights reserved. No part of this publication may be reproduced, stored in a retrieval system, or transmitted, in any form or by any means, electronic, mechanical, photocopying, recording, or otherwise, without the written prior permission of the author.

Printed in Victoria, BC, Canada.

ISBN: 978-1-4269-2733-1 (sc)

We at Trafford believe that it is the responsibility of us all, as both individuals and corporations, to make choices that are environmentally and socially sound. You, in turn, are supporting this responsible conduct each time you purchase a Trafford book, or make use of our publishing services. To find out how you are helping, please visit www.trafford.com/responsiblepublishing.html

Our mission is to efficiently provide the world's finest, most comprehensive book publishing service, enabling every author to experience success. To find out how to publish your book, your way, and have it available worldwide, visit us online at www.trafford.com

Trafford rev. 02/19/2010

Trafford PUBLISHING® **www.trafford.com**

North America & international
toll-free: 1 888 232 4444 (USA & Canada)
phone: 250 383 6864 • fax: 812 355 4082 • email: info@trafford.com

My family is my strength and passion. Bryan, I have grown in your love and unwavering support. Haley, you have been my biggest fan and yes, you too can be an author. Harrison, you are mommy's favorite superhero. I also thank the Raleigh Galloway training program and Bernard Mitchell. Without their support, I would have never attempted nor succeeded in running a full marathon.

PREFACE

As a young and naive college student, I verbalized to my running partner that I wanted to one day run a marathon. Following college, however, I got married and had two wonderful children. I became consumed with motherhood and maintaining a full-time career. I completely stopped exercising and fell victim to convenience foods. By the age of 32, I was an unfit and overweight woman. With the support of my husband, however, I lost 40 pounds on the Jenny Craig program and took back my life. I began to eat healthy and walk daily. My daily walking then gradually evolved into training for my first 5K run. At the end of the run, I then began training for my first Sprint triathlon. I learned that setting fitness goals kept me working out even on the days when personal motivation was low.

At 36 years of age, I felt that I was in the best shape of my life. I was exercising 5 days a week by running, swimming or cycling. Although my runs never exceeded 3 miles, I decided to pursue one of my most ambitious lifetime goals ever—running a marathon. This book provides a week by week summary of how I progressed from running 3 miles to 26.2 miles. I highlight the most important fitness lessons learned each week. Most of the literature available in book stores is written from the perspective of expert marathoners. Their insight is invaluable, but when one becomes an expert, they lose the perspective of achieving running milestones for the first time. This book captures the novice experience and can be a valuable reference for runners that are beginning to train for their first marathon or who feel stuck at the 3 mile distance. With the right guidance and training, you too can progress to reaching your running goals – even potentially running your first marathon.

TABLE OF CONTENTS

List of Tables

INTRODUCTION

This book provides guidance to those currently running short distances to help them gradually increase their running distance. While taking you on one person's journey to completing a marathon, it discusses the Jeff Galloway run/walk program, the benefits of running in a group, running gear/attire, running supplements, adequate fluid replacement, common running injuries and eating for exercise activities over 3 hours duration.

MIND

Background

I met my future husband when I was a junior in college at UNC Chapel Hill. Over the last 13 years, we have created a "bucket list" of things that we would like to do in our lifetime. Our mutual list includes raising children and taking a scenic tour out west to visit many of the state and national parks. I knew that he was the one for me the moment that he agreed that his ultimate vacation destination was Alaska. Some of my individual life goals include learning to scuba dive and riding a Harley on a scenic route. One of the most ambitious goals on my personal aspiration list is to run a marathon. At the time of stating that lifelong goal, however, I didn't even know the true mileage of a full marathon. While in college, I was running regularly with one of my college roommates, Suzanne, and loving the adrenaline rush of running on Chapel Hill's campus. When I learned that a full marathon was 26.2 miles, I assumed that I would never complete that lifetime goal. Furthermore, when I became consumed with motherhood and thus completely stopped exercising, I even wondered if I would ever be physically fit again.

At the age of 32, I was a size 12-14, 179 pound, 5'6" mother of a 5 year old daughter and 3 year old son working as a Family Nurse Practitioner in Cary, North Carolina. According to the BMI (body mass index) charts, I was overweight and close to obese. Since I was not following a healthy lifestyle myself, I often felt hypocritical counseling my patients to improve their health by eating better and exercising. During that time, dinners were often quick and easy–boxed macaroni and cheese with ham; hot dogs with chips; or pasta with butter, processed chicken tenders and green beans. It was about getting dinner to the table and completing the other necessary tasks of the day instead of preparing a nutritious family meal. I pretty much bought all my clothes at Target or Wal-Mart out of convenience. If something didn't fit once tried on at home, I could easily return the items to the store. Shopping in the malls for clothes was not a pleasant experience both due to my weight and having to tote along 2 small kids.

As a consequence of our busy and processed lifestyle, I was at least 30 pounds heavier than my pre-marital weight. My husband had gained weight as well. In the fall of 2006, he was ready to change his ways. He saw advertisements for the Jenny Craig program and decided that he wanted to give it a try. To show support, I too joined JC. I knew that we would both be more successful if we did the program together. I half heartedly started the program, but none the less, strictly adhered to the diet regime. I lost 1-2 pounds consistently for the first few weeks but then reached a plateau during the 4th week. Hoping to spur on more weight loss, I then started walking each morning. My personal rule was that I had to walk for 30 minutes on every work day. If it was a holiday or a vacation day, I did not have to exercise. Over the next 4 months, I achieved my initial JC goal of getting my weight down to 150 pounds. I then continued the program to lose an additional 5 pounds to further tone down my abs. It felt good to be the mother of 2 young children wearing a size 8-10 and looking good in a bikini again. Shopping for clothes was no longer a chore to be completed. Now everything looked good on my new body. I felt youthful and alive.

In my new found youthfulness, I decided to begin running. I wanted to again experience the adrenaline rush of my college running days. I set a goal of running my first 5K in the next 3 months. The first mile that I ran on a treadmill, however, was not an adrenaline rush at all. It was more like a sweat filled, out of breath, exhausting kill joy with side stitches! How could that have happened? I followed the training as recommended on a website specifically for novice runners. I walked ½ mile, ran a mile and then walked another ½ mile. But…I ran at 5 mph having not run in 15 years! How naive. Even with a bad first run, I stuck with the training program of increasing my running mileage by ½ mile each week while continuing the ½ mile walk both before and after the run.

As I lined up for my first 5K, I recall how impressed I was by the well defined bodies of many of the other runners. I wondered who was running the 5K versus the 10K. I even questioned why anyone would want to run a 10K. I was so eager to start the run that I lined up right on the starting line. When the siren blew, I headed out in a blistering pace with the front of the pack. It felt great to get going and I was full of adrenaline. After only one song on my I-POD, however, I was already out of breath. I kept plodding along and kept pace with the group, but stopped cold at the 1 mile water station. After that, I came to the realization that I needed to slow down my pace in order to finish the race. With a much slower pace, I reinitiated my run. Since I had no clue of the race path, I had no idea how close I was to the finish line. The only thing I had to go by is the knowledge that I could typically run 3 miles on a treadmill in 30 minutes. Nonetheless, I kept putting one foot in front of the other. Close to the 2.5 mile mark, I walked 2 blocks to regain my strength. As I looked toward the horizon, I could see what looked to be the finish line. On July 5th, 2008, I completed my first 5K in Wilmington with a time of 28:24.

Training for that race helped me realize the need for personal goals to keep me motivated to continue regular exercise. Weeks later, I experienced a new level of adrenaline rush during my first spin class. This prompted me to set my next exercise goal to combine both running and biking. I signed up for an indoor Sprint triathlon at my local gym. I continued running 3 miles, 3 days a week, typically on a treadmill at the local YMCA, but then added a day of lap swimming and stationary biking to my previous routine. Swimming a full length of the pool was difficult at first, but I progressively worked up to swimming slowly for a full 10 minutes. I even took individual swim lessons to improve my swim technique and learn how to do proper flip turns without getting water up my nose. The biking part was easy given my now routine hour long spin class each week led by perfectly fit monsters! Two months into my training, I started to combine all 3 exercises in succession during a longer Saturday morning work out.

After 3 months of training, I completed my first indoor Sprint triathlon on March 8, 2009. I started the race extremely nervous and excited. I could feel my heart racing even prior to getting into the pool. Having started the triathlon with and elevated heart rate, I had a hard time with each successive lap in the pool and thus only completed 7 lengths of the pool in the allotted 10 minutes. After getting myself together while changing clothes in the locker room, I then pushed hard for 15.9 miles on the bike in 30 minutes and then 2.54 miles on the treadmill in the 20 minute run. Overall, I was disappointed with my swim distance, but pleased with my bike and running distances. I vowed to continue swimming to ultimately improve my overall swimming distance and conquer my pre-race fast heart rate.

I thought about setting the goal of completing a longer triathlon, but I was not mentally or financially prepared to train for biking on the open road. I knew, however, that I needed to set another exercise goal to help keep me motivated to get to the gym on those not so energetic days. Plus, by this time, many of my patients were asking me what I planned to do next.

I can honestly say that Bernard, the Security Officer in our building at work, is the one who ultimately motivated me to run a marathon. Every day upon returning from my lunch time workout, Bernard is there to offer a friendly smile and a word of encouragement. After some time, he asked if I had ever thought about running a marathon. Then his statements became more specific, "you should run a marathon. I think you would do great." He told me about his daily 15+ mile runs on the busy Blue Ridge Road in Raleigh. He shared with me his joy of completing the Boston marathon and running the Marine Corps Marathon amongst soldiers carrying the American flag. He showed me his most prized medals. At the completion of every conversation, he again stated that I would do great running a marathon. Eventually, I confided in him my lifetime goal to complete a marathon. I knew that I needed to set a new exercise goal and Bernard was compelling me to run a marathon. I knew that I was the healthiest that I had ever been and thus rationalized that, if I was ever going to complete my lifetime goal of running a marathon, I should do it now. Plus, I also realized that I could use Bernard to guide and support me through the process.

Setting a Goal

As I inched closer to declaring my next fitness goal, I still had reservations about training for a marathon. How would I progress from running 3 miles to 26.2 miles? How many days a week would I actually need to run? Could I continue to swim and ride a bike to vary my workout routine? How much should I drink and how should I eat to stay appropriately hydrated and nourished during the longer runs? Where would I run the longer distances? Would it be safe to run long distances for hours alone? I checked out a few books at that public library to seek answers to my questions. One of the books that I read was by Jeff Galloway on his run/walk program. I was intrigued that both novice and experienced marathon runners achieved their marathon goals by following his program. Furthermore, I was amazed that the experienced runners often improved their run times by incorporating walking into their running program. I had reservations about whether or not I would feel the same sense of satisfaction with run/walking a marathon as I would with continuously running a marathon. Then I thought, heck it would still be completing a marathon, but hopefully with use of the walk/run method, I would cross the finish line with my head held high and without falling to the ground in exhaustion.

Feeling that I still wasn't set up with all of the elements needed to train for a marathon, I begin a web search to find local running groups. To me, running with a group seemed more appealing and safer, especially when considering training for a marathon. Furthermore, I knew that it would help me feel accountable to someone other than myself when it came to completing the scheduled runs. On May 21, 2009, I came across a website for the Raleigh Galloway training group. Ironically, the group was having their first meeting of the season the following weekend. I read all of the information on the website and felt all of my reservations melt away. I was empowered by the concept of training with a group and being able to do so at my current running pace. I felt a sense of security that I would be guided by group members that had run numerous full and half marathons. I immediately emailed my husband, who was in Canada on a business trip, that I wanted to delay traveling to my parent's house that Saturday so that I could attend the orientation session on the Galloway training program. I was surprised when he quickly emailed his response that he would support me with my training 100%. I don't think that he was surprised at all with my desire to join a team to begin training for a marathon. I think that he was relieved that I would not be running alone and that I would be utilizing the experience of others to guide my training.

I was so excited about the prospect of what was about to happen that on the eve of the orientation meeting, I was not able to sleep. I recall seeing 4:30, 5 and 5:30 am on the alarm clock. I felt like a kid waiting for Santa. I was glad to finally get ready and head towards Raleigh at 8am on May 23, 2009. Throughout the orientation session, I felt like I was at a Mary Kay meeting. I was ready to buy any product and sign up to sale anything. Within the next hour, all of my initial concerns about marathon training were put to rest. I could continue to run 3-4 miles during my weekday runs and gradually progress the number of miles ran on the weekend. My cross-training days could still entail swimming and biking, although aggressive spin classes would need to be put on a temporary hold. I would run with the security of my pace group comprised of both males and females. I would gradually test different water and food intake methods during the longer runs to see which works best in my system. I would utilize the knowledge of my teammates and Jeff Galloway to guide my training efforts. Ultimately, I was sold on the idea of putting forth a lot of time and effort to accomplish a life long dream. I was going to complete my first marathon!

The following day, I made the ultimate declaration of my intent. I stated on my Face book page that I was beginning to train for a marathon. My college running partner, Suzanne, said "You go girl." My friend Stella said, "Wow! What an achievement that would be! That would truly set you apart from us humans!" I also told Bernard of my new commitment. He continued to show his support and stated that he would be there to see me run my first marathon. Now every time I run, I think about how it is going to feel to cross the finish line on November 1, 2009 having completed my first marathon, the Raleigh City of Oaks marathon. I hope that my journey will prove inspirational to my young children, my patients, working moms and novice runners with aspirations and dreams such as my own. I am a typical mom, wife and daughter; yet I aspire to do what only 1% of the population has done. I plan to push myself to my limits and smile upon the completion of my goal. I plan to take in the words of strength and advice from those around me and use those words to guide me through the valleys of my training. Recently Bernard told me the following: "I feel like people go through seasons in their lives. Back when I was running my marathons, it was my season. Now, I feel it is your season. You're gonna do great!" This is my season. It is time for me to do for me. My mind is made up. With the support of my family, friends and teammates, I am going to complete a full marathon.

BODY

TRAINING WEEK 1

Once my mind was ready, I knew that I needed to get my body ready. I decided that I would follow Jeff Galloway's training program as closely as possible. I would continue to workout each work day during my lunch hour and train each Saturday with the Raleigh Galloway training group. My plan was to run for 30-45 minutes each Monday and Wednesday; swim each Tuesday; walk, bike or do yoga on Thursday; and perform the progressively longer runs each Saturday. Fridays and Sundays would be reserved for rest.

My first "official" training day was Memorial Day, 2009. Again I was eager to get started and thus had a hard time sleeping during the night. I set out for a solo run when, one song into the run, my I-POD died. I had grown so accustomed to running with music that I was not sure how I would keep moving. Determined to complete my planned work out, I started paying close attention to keeping my breathing. I found myself relaxing into each running stride. I listened to the bird's spring songs and found myself taking in the sights of nature surrounding me. I thought about how blessed I am to have my health, live in a good neighborhood and have a supportive family. I felt myself getting stronger with each step. Upon completing my 3 miles in 30 minutes, I felt as if I could have kept going for many more miles.

The following day, Tuesday, I was so busy at work that I did not think that I would be able to exercise at all. Swine Flu had hit Durham County and I needed to evaluate 2 patients for possible exposure to the virus. I feared the paperwork alone would occupy a lot of my time. Fortunately, I was able to break free for a quick swim. Unfortunately, however, I was so stressed out with the hectic events of the morning that I had a hard time focusing on my breathing while swimming. I completed 500 yards in the pool, but felt that I was expending a lot of energy. I wish I could have erected a mental wall between my work day and my workout, but I couldn't. Thus, I did not feel a great sense of satisfaction upon completing that day's exercise.

With the previous day's workout being somewhat of a disappointment and knowing that I would be working through my normal lunch/workout hour in order to take my daughter to a special track-out camp, I set an ambitious workout goal for Wednesday. I was going to wake up at my normal time and conquer the entire hill on the road close to my home. Previously, I would stop mid-way on the hill at 1.5 miles out and head back towards home. I knew that running the entire hill would equate to about a four mile run. That, too, would be a first. To make it even harder, I wanted to diverge from the Galloway training and run without walking breaks. I wanted to run without watching the face of a watch for time. With such high aspirations, I started the run a little faster than I should have and thus had to work to complete the last 0.5 miles. Ultimately, however, I accomplished what I set out to do! I took that hill and imagined the pavement caving under my feet with every step. Now, each time I drive that hill in my mommy van, I relive my new respect for the hill and myself.

Having worked so hard the previous day, I decided to take it easy on Thursday. My daughter and I took our puppy for a 1.7 mile walk early that morning. The walk was much slower than my normal walking pace in order to accommodate Haley and Ruffles' pace. When Haley was younger and I was on the Jenny Craig program, she would often awaken early when I was planning to walk; thus, I would cover her from head to toe, strap her into the rickety umbrella stroller and take her with me on my walk as planned. She loved to "walk" so much that she would often ask, "Mommy, can I go walk with you tomorrow." It is really nice on occasion to share my workouts with my daughter.

It provides us with one-on-one time to catch-up and talk about girl stuff. Though she doesn't know it, it is also a time for me to assess the issues currently affecting her life. Furthermore, it is a time to set a positive example for her. I like her to see me exercise and know that I take time to care for myself. I have a quote in my office by Christiane Northrup that reads, "You cannot give real nurturance to another from an empty cup" (Martin, 2008). I often share this quote with my patients to encourage them to take time for themselves. I, too, realize that if I take care of myself, I will be setting an example that other's may hopefully follow.

Friday was a predetermined day for no exercise. The following day, I was both eager and nervous as I drove up to the location of the first Saturday run with the Raleigh Galloway group. I had no clue how to pick the appropriate pace group. I also had no idea of what the terrain or path of the run course was going to be like. I feared that I may not be as strong of a runner as I thought myself to be. Even though running 3 miles was my norm, I worried that I wouldn't be able to complete the planned 3 mile course. I asked one of the group leaders what pace group I should join given that I typically run a 10 minute mile. She recommended the 10:30 or 11 minute pace group and stated that I may need to go to an even slower group. I'll admit, I again felt that I was over-inflating my abilities, but decided to hedge my bets and join the 10:30 pace group.

When the run finally began, I settled into the pace and the run/walk groove. Due to nerves and good conversation, I ended up talking to various members of the group throughout the run. Before I knew it, the run was over. I did make it and I still had energy to boot! I felt that the pace was a little slow, but I realized that running my typical 3 miles with one minute walk breaks every 3 minutes should be easier than my typical running without interruption. I began to look forward to the next week's 4 mile run. Now fully emotionally committed to the training regime, I took a huge step towards declaring myself as a longer distance runner – I purchased my first water belt. I couldn't imagine running with a belt around my waist containing bottles of sloshing water, but I knew that it was in my best interest to get accustomed to wearing the belt and timing my water replacement.

I completed my first week of training by telling my daughter that I was going to run a marathon. I feared that she would be upset since the marathon would be on her 8th birthday. Instead of getting upset, she stated, "Win it mommy!" I explained to her that mommy would not be running to win the race, but to complete the marathon. Like many non-runners, she likely did not understand that a full marathon is a grueling 26.2 miles. She did not understand that mommy was preparing to run over 4 hours in order to cross the finish line. It is not a goal to be taken lightly. After my first week of training and group run, however, I again realized that I was well equipped and on my way to accomplishing my goal.

Key points this week:

1. It is not the end of the world if you are forced to run without music. It actually gives you the opportunity to get in touch with your body and environment.
2. Christiane Northrup states, "You cannot give real nurturance to another from an empty cup" (Martin, 2008). Make time to take care of yourself.

	Monday	Tuesday	Wednesday	Thursday	Friday	Saturday	Sunday
Date	5/25/09	5/26/09	5/27/09	5/28/09	5/29/09	5/30/09	5/31/09
Goal	Get Started	Swim	Run	Walk	Rest	Run with group	Rest
Duration	30 min	25 min	32 min	30 min		35 min	
Distance	3 miles	1000 meters	3.5 miles	1.7 miles		3 miles	
AM pulse	---	---	---	---	---	---	
Weather	Cloudy	NA		Cloudy		Cloudy	
Temperature	69°	NA	65°	65°		65°	
Time	6:24 am	12:10 pm	6:10 am	6:15 am		7:10 am	
Terrain	Sloping	NA	Hills	Slight hills		Flat	
Run/Walk	Run only	NA	Run only	Walk only		3:1	
Rating	9	4	7	8		10	
Comments		Stress hindered workout	Started out too fast	Slow, but cool to walk with Haley		Chose 10:30 Galloway group	

Table 1-Training Log Week 1

Training Week 2

I started my second week of training off with a bang. I had a good meeting with the Durham County Commissioners and realized that they were very supportive of the clinic in which I work. I directed the positive energy received from that meeting into my lunch run. I then realized, however, that I should have held back just a little and complied with the walk/run program. Instead, I ran all out and only took two 30 seconds breaks. Boy...that was stupid! Some of the best lessons are learned the hard way.

The following day, work was so busy that I didn't have time to break free for lunch. That evening, I spontaneously decided to ask my husband to take the kids to bed by himself so that I could go for a walk. He obliged. Since it was 8 pm and I didn't want to get too hyped up before my normal bedtime at 10, I decided to walk an easy 2 miles up to and back from my daughter's school. It was a very nice night and the walk was exactly what I needed. I even came back home and did a 10 minute abdominal workout. It felt good to add some variety to my routine.

Summer came early to North Carolina those first few weeks of June, 2009. Temperatures were consistently in the mid 90's for days. My scheduled Wednesday run fell on a humid day with a high midday temperature. Months prior, I was consistently running in a temperature controlled gym on a treadmill. I had never attempted to run outside in the extreme heat. It seemed more like punishment than pleasure; thus, I avoided it like the plague. However, if I was to continue to follow my planned training program, I would need to weather the elements and run in the heat. I chose to follow Jeff Galloway's recommended slower pace for higher temperatures by running "30 sec per mile slower for each 5 degrees of temperature increase above 60°F (2007, pg 10)." I intentionally started my run at a 13 minute per mile pace. I strictly adhered to the 3 minute run and 1 minute walk cycle. I was able to complete my typical 3 mile run in 40 minutes feeling pretty good, but still preferred to run at an ideal temp of 65°F. Upon entering the building after the run, I encountered my buddy Bernard. He was impressed with my tenacity.

It felt great the next day to get into a cool indoor pool. It was a welcomed break from the heat. I swam nonstop for 500 yards in 10 minutes and felt GREAT! That workout scored a perfect ten on my workout grading scale. It made me think again about incorporating swimming into my next training goal. Again the thought of completing a full triathlon or improving my previous Sprint triathlon swim time entered my mind.

After a day of rest, I was mentally and physically ready for my second group run and first magic mile. The magic mile is a Galloway training tool used to help one determine a realistic race time (Galloway, 2007). The weather was a perfect 65°F; thus I knew that the temperature would not impede my pace. After a 2 mile warm-up run, we began timing the magic mile. I approached the first half of the mile with a very comfortable running pace, but as I passed the next 2 quarter mile markers, I progressively increased my pace. By the end of the mile, I was at a full sprint. I was ultimately impressed that I was able to run my first magic mile in 8 minutes and 30 seconds. I had never run that fast! I then completed the 4 mile run with the usual 3:1 run/walk ratio. Many of us were full of adrenaline from the magic mile and started discussing how many runners or distance athletes have type "A" personalities. At on.wikipedia.org/wiki/Type_A_and_Type_B_personality_theory, Wikipedia describes such individuals as… "inpatient, excessively time-conscious, insecure about their status, highly competitive, over-ambitious, business-like, hostile, aggressive, incapable of relaxation in taking the smallest issues too seriously." It also describes such individuals as "stress junkies." Well…that shoe fits. Only time conscious, competitive and overly ambitious people would ever choose to tackle and succeed in accomplishing the daunting goal of completing a full marathon.

Upon getting home and further processing my magic mile time, I questioned if I was running in the correct pace group. I turned to my Galloway training program book for an answer. According to Galloway's formula for a marathon pace (2007), I can predict that I will run just over 11 minutes per mile in my first marathon. That would have me completing the full 26.2 miles at 4.825 hours. Yuck! Even Oprah completed her first marathon in a faster time! Even with a realistic 5% improvement during the training process, I could only anticipate reducing my overall time to 4.485 hours. What a killjoy! Even with a little deflation of my previously inflated ego, however, I opted to stay with my 10:30 pace group to reduce the possibility of injury or pushing too hard too fast. I also gained a better idea of what I was working toward. Not only am I going to complete a marathon, but I am going to do it in less than 5 hours. Thank goodness, I am on pace to complete the marathon prior to the closing of the race course at 6 hours.

Key points this week:

1. Always start off a run at a slower pace. If you have energy let at the end of the end, you can then run all out!
2. Jeff Galloway recommends running "30 sec per mile slower for each 5 degrees of temperature increase above 60°F (2007, pg 10)."
3. The magic mile can be useful in helping one predict a realistic race time. This is done by warming up with a comfortable 2 mile run and then running the next mile as fast as possible. The time for the fastest mile can then be used to estimate a specific race time. Realistically, that estimated can improve up to 5% with the proper training.

	Monday	Tuesday	Wednesday	Thursday	Friday	Saturday	Sunday
Date	6/1/09	6/2/09	6/3/09	6/4/09	6/5/09	6/6/09	6/7/09
Goal	Run	Exercise	Run	Swim	Rest	Run with group	Rest
Duration	30 min	40 min	40 min	30 min		40 min	
Distance	3 miles	2 ¼ miles	3 miles	700 yards		4 miles	
AM pulse	---	---	---	---		---	
Weather	Low humidity	Nice	HOT!!!	---			
Temperature	85°		90°	---		65°	
Time	11:45 am	8:00 pm	11:45 am	12:10 pm		7:00 am	
Terrain	Slight hills	Slight hills	Slight hills	---		1 hill	
Run/Walk	Run only	Walk only	3:1	---		3:1	
Rating	7	10	8	10		10	
Comments	Started out too fast for a HOT day!	Found a way to get in exercise, added 10 minutes of abs		Swimming rocks!		Magic Mile in 8:30	

Table 2-Training Log Week 2

Training Week 3

My third week of training continued in very hot and humid temperatures. I started the week with a 3 mile run in sweltering 90 degree heat. Even though I followed the run/walk ratio, I found it hard to complete the run. I ran with my "I am a distance runner" water belt and took a good sip of water ever other walk break. I found myself wondering if I was truly hydrating myself well. As a Nurse Practitioner, I knew by education that I was well hydrated if my urine was clear; however, I wondered what fluid replacement I would need in order to maintain good hydration throughout the longer runs. I also wondered when I should begin to replace electrolytes during long runs. Even though this run was only a 6/10 on my personal satisfaction scale, I continued to look forward to the experience and lessons learned from my next run. I also began to seek out answers to the questions that I pondered while running.

The following day, I hit the pool for my now typical 500 yard warm-up in 10 minutes. I swam 300 more yards of random strokes to complete a 25 minute workout. I again found myself really enjoying the swim and feeling a great sense of personal satisfaction upon completing the workout. As a freshman in high school, I tried out for the swim team, but quit after only 3 days of practice. I thought that swimming was too hard and that I would never be good enough to compete against my peers. Thus, I became the "Equipment Manager" for the team. By the end of the season, I watched my friends who were also novice swimmers evolve into good swimmers. One of my friends even started winning some of her events. I had never before quit anything. I vowed that in the future, once I set my mind to doing something,

I would not be a quitter again. I knew that swimming would ultimately help work all aspects of my body while improving my physical stamina and breathing during exercise (VO_2); thus, swimming was a good adjunct to running.

On Wednesday, June 10, 2009, I set out for another run on an extremely hot day. Again, it was a humid 90 degrees. I didn't look forward to running again in the heat, but I knew that doing so would ultimately improve my stamina. I donned my geeky water belt and hit the road. This run was just as hot as Monday's run and I ran the same 3 mile course, however, I felt better at the end of this particular run. I was glad to walk into my office building door and be greeted by Bernard's smiling face. His words to me that day will forever rest on my heart. He said, "I am going to tell you something important. I feel that we all have seasons in our life. Back when I was running marathons – that was my season. Now, it is your season. You're gonna do great!" His words brought tears to my eyes and rendered me speechless. I did finally whisper my thanks and give him a big sweaty hug. One day, I hope to let Bernard know just how encouraging he has been to me in this process. He has been my inspiration and now I hope to inspire others. The situation reminds me of the wonderful movie "Pay It Forward." Oh what a wonderful world this would be if we all took those special occurrences in our lives and used then to benefit others.

That evening, Haley had her first time trials at swim team. My little girl, that was previously not putting her head into the water while swimming, was now swimming freestyle with proper side to side breathing technique. She was also swimming breaststroke, backstroke and butterfly very well. I was so proud to see her accomplishments in action. Unlike me in high school, she stuck it out during those first hard weeks and developed a capacity for swimming. Like Bernard, she too motivates me. That day, I decided that in addition to completing my first marathon, I was going to write a book about my journey. Most of the books available in the library and bookstore are written by experts and fail to fully capture the novice experience. I didn't feel that my experiences were distinctly unique, but typical of a busy, working mom and novice runner. I wanted to document my experiences and praise those who encourage me throughout the journey. I also wanted others to be able to learn from my experiences and thus potentially avoid some of the pitfalls of transitioning from a novice to an experienced runner. Lastly, I wanted to motivate others to pursue their dream, whether that dream is to run a marathon or complete another daunting task that requires months of training and/or preparation. During one of our recent heart to heart talks, my daughter revealed to me that she wanted to be an author, an artist or a teacher upon growing up. Knowing that she would be excited for me, she was the first person I told that I was going to write this manuscript. After hearing the news, she beamed from head to toe. I wanted to show her that she too, could write and publish a book one day. She, along with others, can set a goal, work hard to achieve that goal and ultimately attain the desired goal.

The following day, I decided to cycle at the local YMCA. To keep from fatiguing my thighs, I stayed in the saddle and focused more on speed with light resistance. I wanted to stand up and really get aggressive with the ride, but I feared that I would pay the price during my weekend run if I did. Even with the less aggressive approach, I really enjoyed getting on the bike again. I completed the workout with 10 minutes of abs and push-ups for added diversity. Again thoughts of a future triathlon entered my mind.

I took my normal break on Friday. But instead of running with the group that Saturday, I had the privilege of celebrating my Maw Maw's 90th birthday with family. For 24 hours, we prepped and cooked for the event. In all the chaos, I broke from my typical healthy diet and really pigged out. Breakfast was a greasy, butter soaked sausage, egg and cheese biscuit with a large North Carolina sweet tea from Hardees. I continued to graze throughout the morning on grape salad (green and red grapes covered in cream cheese, walnuts and powdered sugar), ham and raspberry cookies only to eat more grape salad with baked spaghetti, green beans, and 2 pieces of cake for lunch. Furthermore, I proceeded to drink my weight in sweet tea. Upon leaving my grandma's birthday party, we drove back home to celebrate my mother-in-law's birthday with a concert at the Coco Booth amphitheatre. For dinner, I again had another serving of grape salad with a chicken kabob and pita bread. Of course, I completed the evening with a piece of her birthday cake. I bet that I consumed well over 3-4 days worth of calories that day and lodged a plaque of fat right in a coronary artery. Yikes!

As we started our drive home after a wonderful but gluttonous day, I stared processing the fact that at 7 am the following day, I would have to mobilize all of the fat from the previous day in my first ever 5 mile run. Furthermore, I would have to run alone. Lastly, I would have to tackle "the hill" midway through the run. I feared that my overindulgence would hinder my ability to have a good run. Fearing the worse, I started the Sunday morning run at a little slower pace than usual and willingly complied with the 3:1 run/walk ratio. My initial thought was to survive the run, but as I progressed farther down the road, I felt a source of power within myself. I felt strong and confident. I found myself experiencing my first "runner's high." I reflected on the fact that I am not the same women that resumed running 3 years ago. I relished on how fit and healthy I had become. I realized that I had gained my new state of health by no longer making excuses for not taking care of myself. Previously, I had used my kids, family or work as reasons for not having enough time to exercise. Once I decided to stop blaming others for my lack of motivation, I found time to take care of me. Now, I was reaping the benefits of my good health. Thou now 35, I feel 20 something and have the same body that I had at the age of 16. I also continue having no known health issues. How wonderful!

Key Points this week:

1. A basic means for assuring good hydration is to be sure that your urine color is clear.
2. Stop using work, kids or family as an excuse for not exercising so that you can reap the benefits from exercise – improved mental and physical health.

	Monday	Tuesday	Wednesday	Thursday	Friday	Saturday	Sunday
Date	6/8/09	6/9/09	6/10/09	6/11/09	6/12/09	6/13/09	6/14/09
Goal	Run	Swim	Run	Bike	Rest	Missed Run	Run
Duration	36 min	25 min	40 min	30 min			1 hour
Distance	3 miles	800 yards	3 miles	?			5 miles
AM pulse	---	---	---	---			---
Weather	HOT!!!	---	Humid	---			Clear
Temperature	90°	---	90°	---			
Time	11:45 am	12:00 pm	12:00 pm	12:15 pm			7:22 am
Terrain	Slight hills	---	Slight hills	Indoors			Hills
Run/Walk	3:1	---	3:1	---			3:1
Rating	6	10	8	9			10
Comments	Not a fun run due to the heat.	Great swim!	I don't like running in the heat!				Ran my first 5 miles by myself.

Table 3-Training Log Week 3

Training Week 4

Since the previous week threw me off schedule a little, my plan for the upcoming week was to get back to normal. Thus, I proceeded to run my typical 3 miles in Downtown Durham during my lunch break on Monday. To be sure that I still had it in me, I chose to run the whole time just like the old days. I stopped twice for water breaks, but found that I was still easily able to run the entire 3 mile course without taking walking breaks. It was also nice to run in the 80 degree weather instead of 90 degree humidity.

The following day, I did my typical 500 yards in the pool. I noticed at around lap 8 that I was starting to sweat. It is truly weird to feel your body sweating while you are submerged in water. Noticing the sweat helped to confirm that I was getting a good cardiovascular workout and thus made me push harder. Upon returning to the office, I ran into Bernard. He stated that he awoke early in the am and ran 11 miles in 1 hour. That would take me over 2 hours. What a killjoy! Compared to him, I am running in slow motion! He told me that he wanted to run the last 6 miles of my November marathon with me to help me complete the race. My thought was that that would be great, as long as he sticks to my pace and not his own.

That evening, I had the pleasure of attending Haley and Harrison's first summer swim meet. Never in my life did I realize the army of people needed to make a swim meet run smoothly. Since I was a new to the whole concept, I not only had to learn my role as a "recorder" but I had to help my kids understand the concepts of main events, heats, kid pushers and clerks of course. I never realized that swimming had its own vocabulary beyond freestyle, backstroke, breaststroke and butterfly. I developed an even greater respect for the sport of swimming. Furthermore, it was great to see all the kids get so excited to see their teammates swimming and ultimately beating the Hammerheads 202:100.

Since the meet didn't end until 10 pm Tuesday evening, I found it hard to get up and going the following day. To make matters worse, I needed to get a full day's work done in an abbreviated schedule so that I could attend my daughter's "Authors Tea" to celebrate the end of first grade. Furthermore, I had to take our Westie to the vet prior to going back to the pool for swim team practice. Even with the craziness of the day, I worked in a very relaxing Yoga session that evening. It was great to vary my workout and focus more on flexibility and breathing. Apparently the kids watched my workout because as soon as it was over, Haley said, "Mom, you did great. And look, I can do that too." She then proceeded to demonstrate a pretty good three point plank position. From that day forward, she started requesting to do Yoga with mommy. Now that was cool!

The humidity returned that Thursday, but that did not keep me from my planned 3 mile lunch run. Instead of being overzealous however, I strictly adhered to the 3:1 run/walk interval. Ultimately, I completed that run feeling great and looking forward to my first 6 mile run on Saturday with the Galloway group. Since Haley was now pushing me to exercise with her, I looked up information on the Triangle's "Girls on the Run" group. I was saddened to find out that Haley would not be able to participate until the spring due to her late birthday; but I was very impressed with the group's focus on character development through running, class sessions and community service projects.

After taking Friday off for physical rest and hydration, I felt prepared for my Saturday group run. I was eager and nervous about running six miles for the first time. I was further concerned when Ron, our group leader, announced that the day's run would involve hills. I feared the worse. Mentally, I decided to focus on my breathing at the onset of the run to assure better stamina for the hills and full distance. To pass the time and solicit advice, I asked other members of the group at what distance they usually start to use electrolyte replacements and what products they prefer to use. Some stated that they used the electrolyte gels, but many found them a little messy and less palatable. Most, however, preferred the "Shot Block" gummies due to their ease of use and variety of flavors. During the run, I decided that I was going to buy a little of both to use during the next long run. I had already decided against the use of Gatorade or similar electrolyte drinks due to the fear of an upset stomach with or without loose stools while running.

Throughout the run, I found myself gradually increasing my pace and easily making it to the top of the hills. To my surprise, I found the run exhilarating! I stayed at the front of the pack and often had to slow down to keep from running ahead of the designated group leaders. I definitely could have run further than the planned 6 miles. I even verbally persuaded another runner to push through the hills to complete the distance. I realized that all those days of running in the 90 degree heat and humidity had just paid off. I had stamina that I didn't know that I had. Even later that evening, I still had a lot of reserved energy; thus I suggested a family walk at a local park. How amazing!

We wrapped up the week with a nice Father's Day at Frankie's in Raleigh. The best part of the day was getting on the bumper boat cars and squirting each other with water. We all belly laughed and finished the ride soaking wet. The tough part of the day, however, was that Bryan said "no" to a short family vacation at Virginia Beach over Labor Day weekend which would have allowed me to run my first ½ marathon and thus further prep for my full marathon. I was bummed, but not defeated.

Keys points this week:

1. Running under tougher conditions such as heat, humidity or hills ultimately improves your stamina and makes you a stronger runner. Approach new conditions wisely, but don't avoid them.

2. When running over 5 miles, you need to consider some form of electrolyte replacement such as a gel, gummies, powder or solution. It is best to try various products during a run to see which works best for you.

	Monday	Tuesday	Wednesday	Thursday	Friday	Saturday	Sunday
Date	6/15/09	6/16/09	6/17/09	6/18/09	6/19/09	6/20/09	6/21/09
Goal	Run	Swim	Yoga	Run	Rest	Run with group	Rest
Duration	32 min	30 min	50 min	36 min		72 min	
Distance	3 miles		---	3 miles		6 miles	
AM pulse	---	---	---	---		---	
Weather	Warm	---	NA	Humid		Warm & humid	
Temperature	80°	---	NA	82°		82°	
Time	12:00 pm	11:55 am	8:30 pm	12:00 pm		7:15 am	
Terrain		---	NA	Sloping		Hills	
Run/Walk	3 walk breaks		NA	3:1		3:1	
Rating	9	10	9	9		10	
Comments				Great run-even with the humidity.	Hydrate for 100° tomorrow.	Running in heat may have paid off.	

Table 4-Training Log Week 4

Training Week 5

The following Monday led to a normal 3 mile lunch run. I even took time to breathe in the scent of a magnolia tree on my path. I missed the push of running with a group, but overall had a good run. The following day, I didn't really want to exercise, much less swim, but I headed to the YMCA as usual. I ended-up swimming 500 yards and felt wonderful. That night was topped off with the kids winning their second swim meet. During the celebration, I was thrown in the pool-clothes and all. I was so hyped up from the meet that I had a hard time getting to sleep that night.

Wednesday would be a little unusual since I was to attend a medical education class all day. Since the class started later than my typical work day, I planned to go for an early morning run. Even with limited sleep, I popped out of the bed at 6:15 and began pounding the pavement. I opted for an easy 4 mile run with good music and no timer for walk breaks. It was a great run! I was amazed at my personal drive to continue completing my work outs, regardless of alterations in my schedule. During the medical classes which focused on COPD, I learned that women have 17% smaller airways than men. This predisposes women to have more complications from COPD than men. That is also one of the reasons why male professional athletes tend to have faster running times than women. Improved aeration to the tissues and organs ultimately leads <u>some</u> men to perform better than women.

My initial plan for the following day was to bike at the gym; however, when I was notified that our clinic hours were going to be reduced from 36 hours a week to 30 hours a week, I became too preoccupied to exercise. Even though fewer hours at work meant more personal time for me and my family, I was concerned that I would not be able to maintain my typical lunch workout schedule. I feared that my schedule would become so busy that I would feel more pressure to work through lunch in order to get everything done to my standards. I knew that it was imperative to continue following a strict training schedule to assure success with completing my first marathon. That day was further marked with the untimely death of Michael Jackson. Even though I was not a huge fan, I have many fond memories associated with the pop singer's most popular songs. For example, I vividly recall watching the "Thriller" video in its entirety and being amazed with the dancing throughout the video. Furthermore, I remember singing "PYT" verbatim with my sister at the top of our lungs into a fake microphone. That was one of the few moments in time when we were in sync with one another.

The following day, I was determined to get some form of exercise, but I knew that I needed to be careful not to overexert myself prior to my first 8 mile run over the weekend. I thus decided to go out for a walk. I planned to use my IPOD as a distraction, but my battery was dead. Fortunately, I didn't need my IPOD since Michael Jackson songs were audible from every passing car.

On Saturday, I again was to attend a medical education class, but I opted to get to the class a little late so that I could run with the Galloway group. The plan was to complete an 8 mile run. At the half way point, I took my first Shot Block. I found the cranberry flavor pleasing and the consistency similar to that of a thick gummy bear. Close to the end of the run, I took another Shot Block. I later discovered that I had only taken one gummy instead of the recommended 3 gummies. Regardless, I was pleased that I had no GI side effects from the product; however, I didn't like that a lot of the product got stuck in my teeth and became very distracting. Upon completing the run, all of us in the group were amazed to complete the run and see that we had actually completed 8.7 miles in 1 hour and 50 minutes. I was so impressed that I ran for almost 2 hours. Never before did I think it possible to push myself to such extremes, but now I was doing so each week without exhaustion.

During that particular run, I talked to many runners about their planned events. I found 2 women that were contemplating running the half marathon at Virginia Beach. Bryan had previously declined the idea since I presented it as a $600-700, 3 day trip in a hotel right on the beach. Maybe he could be sold on a 1-2 day trip with a cheaper room in downtown Virginia or me going with a group of Galloway girls for 1 night only. Somehow, I felt the need to make Virginia Beach happen to ensure that I get exposed to and work through race day jitters prior to running the full marathon. Fortunately, when presented with my new idea, he was again willing to consider making the trip as a family.

Key points this week:

1. Be flexible with your workout routine to allow diversity and adjustments with schedule changed.
2. If you choose to supplement with the Shot Block gummies, the typical dose is 3 to 6 gummies every hour during exercise, not 1 gummy. It has the consistency of a gummy bear. Some prefer this product since it is easily palatable; however some dislike that they take more time to chew.

	Monday	Tuesday	Wednesday	Thursday	Friday	Saturday	Sunday
Date	6/22/09	6/23/09	6/24/09	6/25/09	6/26/09	6/27/09	6/28/09
Goal	Run	Swim	Run	Unable to exercise	Walk	Run with group	Rest
Duration	32 min	30 min	34 min		40 min	120 min	
Distance	3 miles	2000 yards	4 miles		2 miles	8.7 miles	
AM pulse	---	---	---		---	---	
Weather	Warm	---	Great!		Hot	Humid	
Temperature	80°	---	70°			73°	
Time		12:00 pm	6:15 am		12:00 pm	7:00 am	
Terrain		---	Slight hills			Hills	
Run/Walk	3:1	---	Run only		Walk only	3:1	
Rating	8	8	9		6	9	
Comments	Slight right hip and knee pain		Medical education day	Clinic hours reduced to 30 hours a week	Didn't want to overdue it prior to Saturday's run	Tried Shot Blocks for the first time	

Table 5-Training Log Week 5

TRAINING WEEK 6

June ended just like it began with hot humid days in the 90s. My first run of the week was not enjoyable due to the heat, but I made it 3 times around Durham's downtown loop to complete a 3 mile run. The following day, I again did not particularly want to go for a swim, but I surprised myself with 1000 yards in 30 minutes. That Wednesday, Haley was on her first day of break from year-round school. She came to work with me and we went school shopping after completing work at 12:30. Throughout the day, she often asked if we could do yoga that evening. After completing swim team practice, Haley, Harrison and I did 35 minutes of yoga in the living room. Haley was so pleased with her ability to hold many of the positions. Harrison, on the other hand, was a typical four year old that was interested in the movements for about 5 minutes and then flailing around on the floor acting like a Power Ranger.

The following day was the start of a 5 day vacation. I awoke early Thursday to get in a morning run. I chose to run 5 miles and take the hill yet again. During the run, I was well aware of stiffness in my right knee, but that did not hold me back. I was aware of how it was more difficult to run by myself instead of with a group, but that too did not hold me back. I ran 5 miles in 54 minutes and felt great at the end. Late that evening, we started our drive to Holden Beach. Driving through Wilmington brought back memories of running my first 5K on July 5, 2008. I contemplated driving up to Wilmington to run the Trispan 10 K that Saturday, but then realized that the 2009 race was not scheduled until the weekend following our vacation.

While at the beach, I needed to figure out how I was going to accomplish the scheduled 10 mile run. I looked for a Galloway training group in the Wilmington area, but there was not one. The only formal North Carolina Galloway running groups are in Raleigh and Charlotte. I would have to run alone and in an unfamiliar area. I thought about running at the ocean since it would be easy to run 5 miles out and back. Bryan, however, reminded me of how hard it is to run on sand. Thus, after our first day at the beach, we used the van's odometer to scope out a potential 10 mile run. I was pleased that we found a perfectly flat sidewalk path extending 1 block parallel to the beach. I awoke the next day feeling very nervous about running by myself for such a long period of time. Once at the predetermined run site, I started running with an intentionally slow pace. I valued every walk break-knowing that those breaks would help me get through the full distance. I was surprised at the number of early morning runners that I encountered and was pleased when I spotted a women in a pink shirt running at my pace about 5 blocks from me. Unknowing to her, she and I ran "together" from about mile 2 to 4. I found myself disappointed when she stopped running, but I was glad to have fed off of her energy for 2 miles. At the 5 mile mark, I was glad to turn around and begin steps towards completing the run. I found myself reenergized now that I was on the second half of a long run.

About mile 7, however, I began feeling tired and mentally weak. At that point, another women wearing pink stepped into my path wearing the true sign of a longer distance runner – the water belt. She, too, was running at my pace. As I continued my 3:1 run to walk ratio, I found that I would fall slightly behind her during the walking breaks but then catch up with her during the run. How reassuring! That again solidified my belief that the Galloway method would help be become a better and faster long distance runner. That runner also finished her run before me, but she helped me get over a period of fatigue. Ultimately, I was surprised to complete my first 10 mile run in 1 hour and 40 minutes. Afterwards, I was able to enjoy a day on the boat and beach with my family and in-laws; a dinner of steamed shrimp with cucumber salad and fries; and a butt kicking at a game of cards.

Key points this week:

1. Jeff Galloway's walk run method can help you run distances that you never thought possible. Trust the process and you will go far.

	Monday	Tuesday	Wednesday	Thursday	Friday	Saturday	Sunday
Date	6/29/09	6/30/09	7/1/09	7/2/09	7/3/09	7/4/09	7/5/09
Goal	Run	Swim	Yoga	Run	Rest	Run	Rest
Duration	40 min	30 min	35 min	54 min		1:40	
Distance	3 miles	1000 yards	---	5 miles		10 miles	
AM pulse	---	---	---	---		---	
Weather	HOT!!!	---	---	Great!			
Temperature	90°	---	---	68-72°		67°	
Time	12:00	12:00 pm	8:30 pm	6:45 am		6:30 am	
Terrain	Slight hills	---	---	Hills		Flat	
Run/Walk	3:1	---	---	3:1		3:1	
Rating	6			8		9	
Comments	I did not like running in the heat!	Hard day at work		Right knee stiffness		First 10 mile run by myself	Beach time

Table 6-Training Log Week 6

TRAINING WEEK 7

I started my 7th week of marathon training still on vacation at Holden Beach. After my long run at the beach 2 days prior, I had no doubt that I could run for 30-45 minutes by myself at my new found beach path. As usual when an early morning run was planned, I awoke several times in the middle of the night, fearing that I would oversleep and thus miss my run. This time, however, I was awakened more so by the sound of rain pelting the house in which I was sleeping. Again at 4 am, the same sound disturbed my sleep. Briefly, I wondered if I would go for a run in the rain, but then Ron Wahula's habitual statement that "We Run – Rain or Shine" entered my mind. As long as it was safe, I knew that I would be running.

As I got out of the van to make my approach to my running path, I was pleased to only have a gentle mist of rain hitting my face. A few minutes into the run, the mist stopped and the cool beach wind kicked in. That run was definitely one of the coolest runs that I have had in awhile. I ran 3.5 miles in 39 minutes with the standard 3:1 run/walk ratio. I got back to the beach house around 7:30 to find my husband, kids, dog and in-laws still sound asleep. Though short lived, it was nice to have some time to myself. Within the hour, however, everyone was awake and bustling around. We concluded our beach trip with a quick trip to a local water slide. We all had a blast sliding down the water slides and acting like kids. I belly laughed when I came plowing down "lightening" and lost the top part of my bathing suit. Thank goodness for the big, foam mat that I used to shield myself as I repositioned my suit. What a hoot!

The following day, I returned to reality and the need to complete a full week's work in my now shortened 30 hour work week. I was greeted in the office by prescriptions to fill, calls to return, and a full schedule. Even tough I should have stayed at work to catch-up after returning from vacation, I decided to go the gym for my typical Tuesday lunch time swim. Feeling rushed, I started off too fast and had to stop to rest after only swimming 150 yards. Though I regretted my decision to workout instead of working through lunch, I was determined to swim for a full 30 minutes. I thus slowed my pace and swam an additional 500 yards. At the conclusion of my workout, I was in no way content, but I was satisfied that I put in the time and effort.

The following day continued to be very hectic. I knew that even though I only had to work from 8-12:30, I would have a very busy day. My prediction was true. Though behind with my charting, I left work on time to head home. I started cleaning my dirty house in hopes of regaining my sanity. Disorder leads to chaos in my mind; thus, having a clean home would help to relieve some of my distress. That particular day, I was relieved when the kids decided to skip swim team practice and hang out with their friends at our neighborhood pool. After eating my weight in pizza and watching the kids play in the pool, we returned home to complete the day's homework and prep for the following day. Once the kids were in bed, the thought of exercise was far from my mind. Physically, I was exhausted. Mentally, I wanted to eat a pint of ice cream.

Come hell or high water, I was determined to exercise that Thursday. I pushed through my work schedule and set out for a 3 mile lunch run. I had no desire to walk–I was going to run. I was going to run out some of the built-up aggression from the last few days. I ran hard and I ran fast. It felt so good! After that run, I decided to take my unfinished work home to finally get caught up. Even though I hated working at home until 10 pm, it was nice to go into the next work day with a clear head.

Friday was a planned day of rest to prepare for my first 12 mile run on Saturday with the Galloway group. Even though I slept a solid 7.5 hours, I awoke Saturday morning feeling tired. I was surprised and a little energized to get into my van and see a sweet note from my husband wishing me love, luck and encouragement for my run. After getting to the run site and taking our group picture, we headed out to begin the run. This was to be the first week for those planning to run a full marathon to run farther than those planning to run a half marathon. I feared the mental effects of having part of the group stop at 10 miles, while others, including myself, would have to continue an additional 2 miles.

I felt tired and stiff during the first 3 miles of the run. I purposefully didn't talk to anyone. I then settled into the pace and started a conversation with a co-runner. At four miles, I took a Shot Block to assure that I would not cramp during the run. I felt somewhat disappointed at the 5 mile mark when a group leader yelled out that those running 10 miles were now half way. Her cheer was a little better received at 6 miles when the half way remark applied to me. At the 6th mile, my stomach was growling; thus I decided to eat a couple handfuls of the nut mix (almonds, cashews and cranberries) that I had stashed in my runner's belt. That hit the spot without any unwanted side effects. Eight miles into the run, I decided to take a second electrolyte replacement. This time, I tried an orange GU for the first time. I hated the gooey consistency of the product, but appreciated the caffeine hit that came later. From that point on, I felt good. I had no problem heading out for the additional 2 miles, even though the bulk of the group had stopped at the 10 mile mark. Finishing that 12 miler felt good. I again felt strong and in control of my situation. That run rekindled the fire in me, fed my spirit and strengthened my body.

Key points this week:

1. It is nice to run in the rain, seize the opportunity whenever possible.

2. GU has a dosing frequency of one 15 minutes before exercise and 1 every 45 minutes during exercise. It is properly named GU since it has the consistency of goo. Some dislike this consistency, but others like that it is easy to swallow.

	Monday	Tuesday	Wednesday	Thursday	Friday	Saturday	Sunday
Date	7/6/09	7/7/09	7/8/09	7/9/09	7/10/09	7/11/09	7/12/09
Goal	Run	Swim	Too Busy for Exercise	Run	Rest	Run with group	Rest
Duration	39 min	35 min		32 min		12 miles	
Distance	3.5 miles	?		3 miles		2:24	
AM pulse	---	---		---		---	
Weather	Drizzling	---				Cool	
Temperature	71°	---		80°		70's	
Time	6:30 am	12:05 pm		11:50 am		7:10 am	
Terrain	Flat	---		Slight hills		Flat	
Run/Walk	3:1	---		Run only		3:1	
Rating	10	2		9		9	
Comments	Opted to run in the rain	I went too fast and had to stop-terrible swim!		Determined to run		Shelley Lake	

Table 7-Training Log Week 7

Training Week 8

This week started off with an excellent Monday run. There was a slight drizzle falling, but I had a powerful run with great tunes on my IPOD. I felt like a kid playing in the rain. I ran the hills aggressively and only stopped for traffic. I finished the 3 miles in 32 minutes. Due to the summer heat, I often had to slow my running pace to an 11 or 12 minute mile to allow my body to acclimate to the heat. It was reassuring to know that I could still almost average a 10 minute mile.

The following day was another exhilarating workout. I have no idea how many yards I swam, I just know that I swam non-stop for 11 minutes in a very busy pool. Even though it was hectic in the pool, I was so calm and at peace. I could feel the streamline of water off my body with each stroke. Even my flip turns were smooth and effortless. Having had such a bad swim the previous week, it was great to get back to having a great swim.

On Wednesday, I had to run errands after work. Fortunately, those errands were completed sooner than expected and I was left with an hour until I needed to pick up my daughter at the bus stop. I thought about picking up my son early from daycare, but then opted to take the hour for myself and do a session of yoga. It was great to have some time for me; however, I felt that I had to watch the clock throughout the workout session to be sure that I didn't miss meeting the bus. Regardless, I was proud that I had taken some time for myself to nurture my mind and body.

My typical run for Thursday was thwarted by a lunch date to further discuss some clinic issues at work; thus, I needed to get creative with accomplishing my second run of the week. Fortunately, the kids were too tired to go to swim practice that evening and were content with watching a movie at home. Thus, I seized the opportunity to get on the treadmill in my garage for a quick 3 mile run at 6 mph. I was interrupted twice by the kids, but not to the point of having to stop my workout. Knowing that I had my first 14 mile run planned for the weekend, I decided to calculate my sweat rate during this workout to better gauge how much water I should be drinking while exercising. "If you will be exercising for more than three hours, you really should know your sweat rate to prevent the performance decline associated with small cumulative mismatches between how much fluid you need versus how much fluid you are losing via sweat (Clark, 2008, p 152-153)." Losing more than 2% of your body weight during exercise can lead to excessive dehydration. The sweat rate is calculated by weighing yourself nude both before and after a one hour workout. For every pound lost (16 oz), 80-100% of the loss should be replaced during exercise (Clark, 2008). During my 30 minute run in the hot garage, I lost 2.5 pounds of water weight. Thus, during a full hour of exercise in the extreme heat, I estimate that I could lose 5 pounds via sweat. At 139 pounds, that is greater than a 2% weight loss and thus risky for extreme dehydration. I should therefore consume 64-80 oz of water during each hour of exercise. Wow, that is 8-12 bottles of water on my water belt per hour. Impossible! How could I drink that much without having a sloshing feeling in my stomach or having to stop to use the bathroom?

Now realizing the importance of hydration during exercise, I also decided to determine how much water is recommended prior to initiating exercise. According to Clark, "the prehydration goal is to drink about 2 or 3 milliliters per pound (5 to 7 ml per kg) of body weight at least 4 hours before the exercise task (2008, p 152)." Thus, I should drink approximately 8-12 oz of water before exercising. Since my Saturday run was to begin at 6:30, adhering to the 4 hour period before exercise was impossible, but getting that quantity of water in would be feasible.

When Saturday finally arrived, I started the group run a little tired and thus glad to be running with my group. It was great to see familiar faces and know that we would again accomplish milestones together. The first 4 miles were relatively easy, but then boredom set in. I was not sure how I was going to be able to complete the full 14 miles. I thus decided to spur on more conversation with a co-runner to pass the time. Thanks to good conversation, the next 6 miles went by quickly. During the run, I again took one Shot Block at mile 5 and a GU around mile 8, but I also ate 4 fat free Fig Newtons in the middle of the run. All sat well on my stomach.

When starting the final 4 miles of the run, I was amazed with my energy level. Having no group leader to guide us, three of us set out with a Gym Boss timer and Garmin to complete our final mileage. We picked up a stray runner along the way that had no means of measuring his running distance. I had enough energy to pace the group for the first 2 miles and then run alongside a co-runner to the finish. I commented to the group that I could feel my feet tingling while running. It seemed as if my feet were hypersensitive to the cotton threads of my socks. The other runners recommended that I be sure to use sweat wicking running socks or consider wearing my socks inside out. During the final mile, the majority of us had to push through stiff knees and hips to keep moving forward. Ultimately, however, we completed the full 14 mile run in 2 hours and 57 minutes. Wow, I ran for almost 3 hours! After the run, I purchased a different brand of running socks to attempt to reduce the awkward sensations that I began experiencing during the later stages of the run. I also opted to reward myself with a chocolate chip bagel loaded with fat free cream cheese. Once at home, I spent the day hoping to remain still. Any movement, especially climbing stairs, exacerbated the aching in my joints.

During this eighth week of training, I began reading more literature about preparing to run a marathon. I learned that those who take more than 4 hours to complete a marathon are considered "slow marathoners." Heck, that almost 3 hour run didn't feel slow to me. I thus prefer the more flattering term—endurance athlete. Regardless, I decided to begin increasing my carbohydrate intake to better prep for longer runs. According to Nancy Clark, "a daily carbohydrate intake of about 3-5 grams of carbohydrate per pound of body weight (6 to 10 g per kg) prevents chronic glycogen depletion and allows you to not only train at your best but also compete at your best (2008, pg 114)." At 139 pounds, I calculated my daily carbohydrate need as 417-695 g per day. What a change in mindset given that for the last 4 years, I have tried very hard to keep my carbohydrate intake lower to keep off the weight that I had lost with Jenny Craig. Needing further assistance, I began using www.sparkpeople.com to track my daily caloric, carbohydrate, protein, fat and sodium intake as well as my caloric expenditure from exercise (Appendix A and B).

Spark people recommends 1,550-1,900 calories per day for a 5'6" female weighing 139 pounds; however it would be impossible to consume the needed carbohydrates for distance running and stay within that caloric range. Clark (2008) recommends that calories should be adjusted upward for being active throughout the day and for structured exercise. Since I am moderately active throughout the day at work and at home with the kids, I added an additional 50% to my daily resting metabolic rate of 1390 calories per day ((139 pounds X 10 calories per pound) + 695 calories). I also added 400 calories per day to account for exercise. Thus, a more accurate daily caloric intake for me is around 2485 calories per day. Having the basal metabolic rate measured would be ideal and can be accomplished at some facilities for a fee, but using Clark's equation at least provides a gross estimate of my caloric need.

While tracking my dietary intake over 6 consecutive days, I consumed an average of 2243 calories per day. Averaging only 306 carbohydrates in the 6 day period, I consistently fell short of the recommended carbohydrate intake even though I had started purposefully eating more carbohydrates. I exceeded the recommended 40-70 grams of fat with an average of 170 grams consumed daily. Most of this excess fat was due to my indulgence in Trader Joes' dark chocolate edamame. On all days, I consumed protein within the desired range of 60-158 grams a day. Overall, having more thoroughly evaluated my dietary intake, I was able to understand why I am continued losing weight while eating LIKE A PIG! Even though I am eating every 3 hours with at least 3 meals and 3 snacks throughout the day, I am still not consuming the calories needed to maintain my body weight. My diet is so much better than before, but I know that I, as well as other endurance athletes, need to strive to get the proper intake of nutrients to ensure the stamina to train for and complete a marathon. Anyone can benefit from use of tools such as sparkpeople.com to measure caloric intake and expenditure and then make adjustments accordingly.

Key points this week:

1. If you are going to be exercising for more than 3 hours, you need to know your sweat rate. The sweat rate is calculated by weighing yourself nude both before and after a one hour workout. For every pound lost (16 oz), 80-100% of the loss should be replaced during exercise (Clark, 2008).
2. According to Clark, you should hydrate with "2 or 3 milliliters per pound (5 to 7 ml per kg) of body weight at least 4 hours before the exercise task (2008, p 152)."
3. Technical running socks with sweat wicking properties can protect the feet from sweat and friction during a long run. These are readily available at running stores.
4. "A daily carbohydrate intake of about 3-5 grams of carbohydrate per pound of body weight (6 to 10 g per kg) prevents chronic glycogen depletion (Clark, 2008, pg 114)" and allows an athlete to train at their full potential.

5. The website sparkpeople.com can be an invaluable tool in helping track and improve nutritional intake and caloric expenditure.

	Monday	Tuesday	Wednesday	Thursday	Friday	Saturday	Sunday
Date	7/13/09	7/14/09	7/15/09	7/16/09	7/17/09	7/18/09	7/19/09
Goal	Run	Swim	Yoga	Run	Rest	Run with group	Rest
Duration	33 min	30 min	45 min	30 min		2:57	
Distance	3 miles	?	---	3 miles		14 miles	
AM pulse	---	---	---	---		---	
Weather	Drizzle	---	---			Cloudy	
Temperature	73°	---	---	---		70's	
Time	12:05 pm	12:00 pm	2:00 pm	7:30 pm		6:45 am	
Terrain	Slight hills	---	---	Treadmill		Occasional Hills	
Run/Walk	Run only	---	---	Treadmill		3:1	
Rating	10	10	9	7		8	
Comments	I liked running in the rain and ran the hills with power.	Swam calmly in a busy pool	Great Yoga session	Needed to get in exercise		Knee/hip stiffness throughout the day and felt more tired than usual	

Table 8-Training Log Week 8

Training Week 9

My 9th week of training started as usual with a planned lunch run. Feeling more energetic and having more time than usual, however, I decided to run 4 miles instead of my typical 3 miles. I also decided to stray from the norm of running in circles around the downtown loop and instead ran the course in a clockwise and then counterclockwise fashion. It was amazing how such a simple change made the run more interesting. I found myself picking up the pace on mile 3 and sprinting at the end of the 4th mile. I also experienced no tingling in my feet with use of my new, water-wicking running socks. That run was AWESOME! Upon returning to my building, I ran into my buddy Bernard. He was impressed that I had completed 14 miles over the weekend. He compared me to his sister in law that was about 107 pounds and able to complete a marathon in just over 2 hours. That was a flattering, but erroneous comparison.

The following Tuesday, I mentally did not want to do any form of exercise, but I willed myself to the gym for a swim. Again I surprised myself with completing 500 yards in 10 minutes. I continued to swim for a full 30 minutes, even after hitting my forehead on the side of the pool during a flip turn. My strokes felt smooth and I could feel my body gliding through the water. I continue to be amazed with the progression of my swimming ability.

Wednesday was to be a short work day and the first early release day for Wake County Schools. I had no idea how I was going to get my workout in that day, but I initially planned to do yoga with the kids. At the latter half of the evening, however, the kids decided to watch a movie; I thus opted to get on the treadmill in the garage. I found running 3 miles hard on that particular day. I continuously watched the timer and mileage and urged the 3 mile mark to hurry up. I was grateful to complete my needed workout for the day, but disappointed mentally with the experience.

To shake things up a little and get my head back in the game, I decided to go for a spin that Thursday in the gym. It had been a while since I had gone for a spin, and I felt the need for speed with aggressive tunes. During the workout, I was surprised with how conditioned I had become. Previously with the same pace and resistance, I would have been in a sweat by the end of the first song; this time, however, it took three songs to break a good sweat. I got out of the saddle twice and really pumped up the resistance. Ultimately, that was a great workout and a much needed change in the exercise routine.

Due to a family reunion on Saturday, I would sadly have to miss the Saturday group run. The group was planning to do an Indian run or fartlek. A fartlek is a type of speed play used to reduce the monotony of the typical run while working on pace and stamina. For our particular group, the plan was to run in a single file line. The last person in the line would then sprint to the front of the group. This pattern would be repeated throughout the run. When due, a walk break would not start until the sprinter made it to the front of the group. Given that I had only heard of a fartlek, I was sad that I would miss the experience. Even though I would be running a somewhat unfamiliar path the following day, my plan was to attempt to incorporate periods of sprinting into the running session.

My 10 mile solo "make-up" run on Sunday began with the best intentions. My plan was to run a full greenway course approximately 1 mile from my home. I had heard that from my house, the course was approximately 7 miles out and back; thus my plan was to run the distance of the greenway, add part of a local road until the 5 mile mark, and then double back for the final 5 miles. Unfortunately, the good plan went bad. The planned greenway route was only a total of 3 miles from my house instead of 3.5 miles; therefore, I needed at least 2 additional miles on the front half of the run to be able to double back for the full 10 miles. Running alone and having to figure out where to run an additional 2 miles in the midst of fatigue is not pleasurable. Fortunately, I had my husband's I-phone and "Trailguru" to gage my distance. The only problem was that I had to look at the phone screen and continuously monitor my mileage. I ran here, there and everywhere to get in those additional miles. Furthermore, I added an unplanned hill at the 5 mile mark in order to obtain the full 5 mile distance. I was so glad to descend that hill and know that I was finally on the way back home to complete the run. Even though I was very tired at the 4-5 mile mark, I ran comfortably from mile 5-9. The final mile was tough, but I ultimately completed the full 10 miles. Looking at the final course on the I-phone screen made it appear that I had done loop-de-loops throughout Apex. Having completed my predetermined distance, however, gave me a sense of pride in myself. I was proud that I had toughed it out and gone the full distance. I thought to myself that, even if alone during the half or full marathon, I would be able to dig deep within myself to accomplish whatever was ahead.

Key points this week:

1. Simply reversing the direction of a run course can make a routine run more interesting.
2. A fartlek is a type of speed play used to reduce the monotony of the typical run while working on speed and stamina.
3. Finishing a tough run makes you both mentally and physically stronger.

	Monday	Tuesday	Wednesday	Thursday	Friday	Saturday	Sunday
Date	7/20/09	7/21/09	7/22/09	7/23/09	7/24/09	7/25/09	7/26/09
Goal	Run	Swim	Run	Bike	Rest	Missed run with group	Run
Duration	44 min	30 min	30 min	30 min			120 min
Distance	4 miles	?1000 yards	3 miles	?			10 miles
AM pulse	---	---	---	---			---
Weather	After rain	---	---	---			
Temperature		---	---	---			
Time		12:00 pm	Pm	12:00 pm			6:45 am
Terrain	Slight hills	---	Treadmill	Indoors			Rare hill
Run/Walk	Run only	---	Treadmill	NA			3:1
Rating	10	8	7	10			7
Comments	I varied typical run course and had a great run!		I watched the miles and wanted to stop.	What a great spin! Changed caloric intake		Family reunion	I had to come up with route during the run–HARD!

Table 9-Training Log Week 9

TRAINING WEEK 10

Usually my long runs are followed by a day of rest, but since I had to make up a long run on a Sunday during the previous week, I needed to again run on Monday to get back to my normal training schedule. Unfortunately, that run fell on a day in which my assistant called out sick and the hot days of summer returned. I was very behind with my charting and inundated with phone calls, but determined to go for a run. Thus, I dropped everything at 12 noon, changed clothes, fired up my IPOD and headed outside. Knowing that I needed to get back to the office as soon as possible, I chose to run without walking breaks.

I felt really good during the first mile of the run, but I think my mind was clouded with the craziness of the day and the initial adrenaline rush from running. By the second mile, it donned on me how hot and humid it was outside and that I had not brought any water. That was irresponsible, stupid, stubborn, careless and all of the other derogatory adjectives that can be used to describe someone that exercises without being fully prepared. My legs and heart rate were good, but my body was on fire. After the first mile, my hair was already drenched with sweat. I realized that there was no way to safely complete even 3 miles without at least taking rest breaks. I thus took a one minute walk break in a shady area. I noticed that my right knee was feeling more loose and unstable than usual, but it didn't seem to interfere with my running. I debated abandoning the run and just walking the final distance, but then willed my body to run again. I again took another walk break after having to stop for traffic, but then again pushed forward in a run.

I don't think that I have ever been happier to finish a 3 mile run in my life. That was a terrible experience that will likely leave a bad taste in my mouth for some time to come. Had I been wiser and stuck to what I had learned through the Galloway training program, I would have followed the 3:1 run/walk routine, slowed my pace for the hotter weather, and definitely ran with water. Furthermore, I would have given myself a lighter workout having just completed a 10 mile run on the previous day. I guess the best lesson is that now the lesson is learned!

The following day's workout started out as usual, but mentally I stopped swimming after only completing 400 yards in the pool. I felt that my body was weak. Once I started having the slightest fatigue, I began reflecting on the previous day's bad run and was therefore unable to focus on my breathing while swimming. I managed to swim for a full 30 minutes, but again, my workout was more discouraging than encouraging. I decided that I would thus take the next day off from exercise to enable my body and mind to rest.

On Wednesday, instead of exercising, I went to my primary care physician's office for pain in my throat. I wasn't sure if I was having reflux or problems with my thyroid. Ultimately, I was reassured that I was likely only having reflux. I later deducted that the problem stemmed either from my now increased carbohydrate intake of 417-695 grams per day or my recent increased consumption of Trader Joe's dark chocolate edamame. Either way, my diet had to change. I not only had daily throat pain with constant clearing of my throat, but I also constantly felt full. I decided that I would continue eating high carbohydrate foods, but that I would try to spread those meals out better throughout the day. I would also stop eating when I felt full. Lastly, I vowed that I had purchased my last tub of dark chocolate endamame... at least for now.

That Thursday, I felt reserved as I headed out for my second run of the week. Due to the humidity, I purposefully started the run at a 12 minute pace. I left my I-pod at the office since I knew that certain tunes would likely quicken my pace. The only sounds that kept my attention were my breathing and my Gym Boss prompting me to run or walk. After every other walk break, I made sure to take a swig of water from one of my 2-8 oz water bottles. I completed the 3 mile run in 36 minutes and had energy reserved to sprint to the finish. What a difference a few days can make! My body needed a break and was now rebounding with energy. I felt as prepared as possible for the planned 16 mile run on the following Saturday.

I was sure to take it easy the following day. I didn't even mow the grass for fear of overexerting myself and negatively impacting my long run the next day. I purposefully ate as many carbohydrates as possible to assure that my glycogen stores were completely full. I thoroughly enjoyed my Chick-fil-A chocolate milkshake and then my Rita's mango Italian ice. In hindsight, however, I may not have drunk enough water that day to adequately prepare me for the hot, long run to follow.

My first 16 mile run started well with the 10:30 Raleigh Galloway pace group. I was mentally prepared for the hilly run and eager to get started. Kristen and I passed the miles with conversation about our last week and our plans for the current weekend. At mile 4, however, I began having a sense of instability in my right knee. I commented to Kristen that it felt like my knee could give way as I was running down hills. All was well on the flat and uphill portions of the run, but the pain was more noticeable on the down hill slopes. Part of the group turned back at the six mile mark since they only needed to complete a 12 mile run that day, but I opted to tough it out for more mileage. Again at 7 miles, I had to decide if I would turn back with the 14 mile group or push forward as planned. Since we were heading into Umstead Park and my November marathon was to take place on those trails, my curiosity of the course keep me going for an additional mile. Even in mild pain, I did not find the notoriously hilly Umstead Park that bad; although, I reserve the right to change my mind after running the entire path in the future.

I was so glad to reach the 8 mile point and turn back to complete the run. I felt a sense of inner confidence since I had pushed through pain to get that far. The next mile was pretty easy, but then my attention turned to concern that all of my water bottles were empty and the next water cooler was about 1.5 miles away. The course was initially set up to be 5 miles out and back with the whole pace group and then a repeat of the same route for an additional 2, 3, or 4 miles out and back to complete a total of 12, 14, or 16 miles, respectively. Each person's distance was based on the event(s) they were planning to run and when these event(s) were scheduled. Since Umstead was not initially part of the running course, water stations were not set up along that path. Out of the seven runners in the 16 mile group, only one runner had water remaining. Fortunately, she offered me a sip and I gladly accepted. Once at the next water cooler, we all took a few minutes to chug down a full 8 oz and replenish our water bottles. We then all slowly reinitiated our run.

I continued having pain in my right knee, but I was mentally prepared to will myself through to the end. I was glad to pass familiar landmarks and take each step closer to the finish. I was still reserved with running down hill, but confident that I would finish the run. I followed my normal electrolyte fluid supplementation, but prolonged the initiation of GU until mile 8 and the completion of my 6 Fig Newtons until mile 10. I took a sip of water during every other walk break. To pass the time, I started a discussion about running the full 26 miles or just 20-23 miles prior to one's first marathon. Although a lot of the books guide you to run a maximum of 23 miles prior to your first marathon, those in the Galloway group were adamant that a novice should run the full 26 miles in training to help him or her get through the final 6 miles of their first marathon. Everyone that I have talked to speaks about "hitting the wall" at around mile 20 of a full marathon. Many agree that having the experience of running the full 26 miles in training helps one ultimately complete the full marathon.

At about mile 13, I began to feel tighter in my right thigh with each successive walk break. I told my group that I was going to walk faster during the walk breaks in order to keep moving briskly and then run slower at the beginning of the run cycles in order to allow them to catch-up. Unfortunately, I continued to feel my right quadriceps muscle getting tighter and tighter. It felt as if my right leg were becoming shorter than my left leg. At about 13.5 miles, I was overcome with a quadriceps cramp. I had to stop. I would have cried, but I couldn't even do that. The pain was comparable to the unrelenting and uncontrollable pain of contractions during labor. Having given birth to a 9.8 pound son naturally, I was well aware of the pain of childbirth without the use of medication. One of the team leaders came to my side to offer words of support and encouragement. After about 30 seconds, I felt that I could again begin to move. I was not able to run at first, but I could walk. Not wanting to fall behind the group, I willed my feet forward. My supportive group slowed their pace for the next 3 minutes and I found the cramp somewhat easing. Cara distracted us all by sharing one of her most embarrassing moments. I was able to walk briskly during the next walk break and then begin a slow jog. I keep putting one foot in front of the other. As the intervals passed, I fell behind some members of the group, but was able to keep them within sight. I was so glad to reach the 16th mile; but even having completed the run, I was not able to stop moving. I again was having a cramping sensation in my right quadriceps muscle. I kept walking for an additional 5 minutes and drank as much water as possible. After a few more minutes, I was able to begin stretching. Only then did I finally have relief of my pain. After that experience, I vowed to never again take stretching for granted. That was by far the toughest run ever. I was so proud that I had completed the running goal for the day, but worried that my knee pain and quadriceps cramp was going to keep me from progressing further.

After the long run, I went to brunch with many of the girls in my running group. We talked about what led us to run, what races we were planning to run and what events we had completed in the past. We also shared personal information with one another. It was a great break from the monotony of just running together. Though we vary in professions and family make-up, we are all goal driven, strong females with a mission to push our bodies to the extreme.

Immediately upon getting home, I ate lunch and took an 800 mg Ibuprofen. As the day progressed, my right knee became stiffer. After dinner, I again took another 800 mg Ibuprofen. I also iced and elevated my knee. The following day, I purposefully avoided any exercise and continued nursing my knee with Ibuprofen and ice. The pain improved, but never resolved. With each basic step, I was well aware of the stiffness and slight weakness of my right knee. I worried that I would not be able to train as needed during the following week. I wasn't sure if I should be completely resting or gently stretching the limb. With each day, the pain was changing; thus, I could not fully isolate the source of the symptoms. Even as a Nurse Practitioner, I did not medically know what I needed to do. Thus, I decided to go to see an Orthopedist to have my injury more thoroughly assessed to ensure that I implemented the correct treatment. For years, I had only seen my health care provider yearly for a routine physical. Now, I was going to have my second medical office visit in 2 week's time. What was happening?

Key points this week:

1. Always check the weather conditions before exercising outdoors and alter your pace, walking breaks, water consumption, or supplements accordingly.
2. Listen to your body and take a break from exercise when needed. Missing one day of exercise will not stunt your progress – it will likely enable you to progress.
3. Endurance athletes need to consume additional carbohydrates each day; however, those additional carbohydrates need to come from complex carbohydrates

such as breads, pastas, rice and potatoes, not simple carbohydrates such as junk food or alcohol.

4. Always be sure to fill up all of your water bottles at every water stop. You never know when the next water station may be further than you think.
5. Don't take stretching for granted. Many novice runners experience injuries due to poor stretching after running.
6. When in doubt about a physical ailment, seek professional help.

	Monday	Tuesday	Wednesday	Thursday	Friday	Saturday	Sunday
Date	7/27/09	7/28/09	7/29/09	7/30/09	7/31/09	8/1/09	8/2/09
Goal	Run	Swim	Rest	Run	Rest	Run with group	Rest
Duration	33 min	25 min		36 min		3:30	
Distance	3 miles	400 yards		3 miles		16 miles	
AM pulse	---	---		---		---	
Weather	Hot & humid	---		Humid!		Overcast	
Temperature		---		91°			
Time	12:00 pm	12:00 pm		12:00 pm		6:45 am	
Terrain	Slight hills	---		Slight hills		Hills	
Run/Walk	Run only	---		3:1		3:1	
Rating	3	5		10		3	
Comments	I had a bad run. I should have used the walk breaks.	Mentally stopped swimming after only 8 lengths due to fatigue.		What a difference a day of rest can make!		CRAMP	Took Ibuprofen and used ice

Table 10-Training Log Week 10

TRAINING WEEK 11

As soon as I got to work on Monday morning, I called to get an appointment with the Orthopedist. At lunch, I decided to go for a swim knowing that such activity would not stress my knee, but could provide both therapy for my knee and a good cardiovascular workout. Even though the pool was exceptionally busy that day, I was very relaxed while swimming. My strokes felt effortless and ultimately I had an amazing swim! I didn't even count my laps, I just kept swimming. My knee felt great while I was in the pool, but when I stepped on dry land, the stiffness was again noticeable.

That afternoon, I was examined at the Orthopedist's office. My knee x-rays were perfectly normal. To my delight, I was told that my knee and hip pain (which he exposed during his exam) was due to a tight IT band. The ligaments in my knee were a little lax or weak, but he attributed that to the fact that I was quickly increasing my running distances. He stated that IT band injuries are more common after a change in shoes, running surfaces or running distances. His perception was that my quadriceps cramp was just that, a cramp. He provided me with handouts on IT band stretching, recommended that I take it easy this week with training, and encouraged me to hydrate better during longer runs. That evening, I implemented all of his suggestions. I began a daily IT band stretching routine. I started monitored my fluid intake more closely. Lastly, I made up my mind that, no matter what, I would not attempt to run again until I could honestly say that I was no longer experiencing pain.

The following day, I opted to go for a spin at the gym. I figured that sitting and cycling would not put additional strain on my IT band and would be a good warm-up prior to thorough stretching. While spinning for 30 minutes, I had no noticeable pain. Mentally, I found it hard to stay in the seat, but I stayed seated none the less. I then did 15 minutes of stretching that incorporated every IT band, patello-femoral, and hip stretch possible. At the end of the workout, I felt great and very limber. Later that day, however, I noticed stiffness of the right knee again. I still found it odd that my pain kept localizing to my knee and not my hip or lateral thigh; however, I felt assured that the problem was the insertion of the IT band on the knee and not a "knee" injury.

As usual, Wednesday was a very busy work day from 8-12:30. I then quickly ate lunch, picked-up Harrison at daycare, drove 40 minutes home, and met Haley at the school bus at 3 pm. Once at home, the race to unpack from the current day, pack for the next day, do homework, wash clothes and cook dinner got underway. After dinner and walking the dog, however, I took time for a hips/thighs/buns yoga routine. I did not particularly like the fast pace of the male instructor, but the lower extremity stretching felt good. By that time, the kids were watching the Cosby Show with my husband, thus I snuck in an additional 10 minute abdominal workout as well. After a hectic day with constant running around, it felt good to take some time for myself and get in a relaxing workout.

Since I had not experienced any knee or hip pain for the last 24 hours, I decided that I would attempt to run at work the following day. Of course, it was supposed to be another August scorcher, but I knew that I could take the heat if I prepared adequately and ran as trained. I set out with a 12 minute per mile pace with 2 fully loaded water bottles and no tunes. I intentionally went a path with more uphill slopes than downhill slopes since downhill running had previously caused more pain. I followed the recommended 3:1 run/walk cycle without exception. The first mile went by without pain. In the second mile, I felt a little loose in my right knee, but still had no pain. In the third and final mile, I was relieved that I still was not experiencing any pain. I was sure to stretch for a good 10 minutes after the run and surprisingly, even that felt good. Although my mind was constantly consumed with the thought and fear of pain, I ended up having a pretty good run that I rated as an 8/10 for enjoyment. I was relieved to feel capable of keeping on track with my marathon training program. I felt confident that I could at least push through the 10 mile run on Saturday.

The following day, I planned to take a break from exercise, but as usual, running was on my mind. I received the Wannabeasts weekly newsletter by email. The newsletter reviewed recommendations for carbohydrate replacement after a long run. Upon finishing the last 16 and 10 mile runs, I craved a bagel and chocolate milk. Come to find out, my body was craving an appropriate carbohydrate/protein snack. The newsletter reviewed that it is recommended to replace ½ grams of carbohydrates per pound of weight within 60 minutes of exercise; however the most effective period for replacement is 15-30 minutes after exercise. Even more optimal is to have a 1:4 protein to carbohydrate snack such as chocolate milk, low fat yogurt with granola, or peanut butter on a whole wheat muffin. The carbohydrates allow glycogen replacement while the protein builds and repairs muscle and thus improves the rate of glycogen synthesis within the muscles. After reading that, I understood why I had been craving a bagel with chocolate milk and knew that my post run snack was a keeper.

Upon awakening on Saturday morning, I was a little apprehensive about running 10 miles. I feared that my knee would hinder my ability to keep up with the group and/or complete the run. I reassured the group that my knee had been evaluated and that I was feeling much better. Kristin told me that, although she had not experienced any pain during the Saturday run, she too started having IT band stiffness during her Monday run. We all reviewed how "beat up" we felt after the 16 mile run the previous week. EVERYONE was commented on how that particular run was the toughest yet. Boy was I glad to hear that. Those were my sentiments as well!

With the reassurance that I was not alone in experiencing the difficulties of the last run, I got moving with what I was hoping would be a pleasant, flat, easy 10 mile run on the Durham portion of the Tobacco Trail. The group seemed more chatty than usual, likely because we weren't running hills and we were well protected from the heat by overcast skies and numerous shade trees. I was sure to drink water with each walk break and continue my typical electrolyte replacement with 3 Shot Blocks at 4 miles and a GU at 8 miles. At around 6 miles, I overheard other runners discussing whether or not they would run the 23 and 26 mile runs prior to their first marathon. Both stated that they had run a full marathon before without running beyond 20 miles in training. Kristen also chimed in that she had not run beyond 20 miles prior to her last marathon. I still felt perplexed about the subject, but decided that I would see how the next 18 and 20 mile runs went prior to making my final decision.

As we continued with the run, I was amazed at how good I felt. I only felt a slight stiffness in the upper right thigh which was nothing in comparison to the previous week's pain. Upon finishing the 10 mile run in 1:55, I felt that, had this been planned for a longer run, I easily could have kept going. I in no way pushed for more mileage, however, since I knew that I would need my strength for the next week's 18 mile run. I calculated that I drank 12-8 oz bottles of water during that 10 mile run. In retrospect, this was not an appropriate fluid replacement based on my previous sweat loss calculations (see Chapter 10). In the 2 hour run, I should have consumed between 128 to 160 ounces of water or 14-20 bottles of water. I would have to see if this poor water intake would lead to further physical woes.

Key points this week:

1. The ligaments supporting the knee can be lax or weak when a runner quickly increases their running distance.

This can lead to some noticeable instability of the knee while running, but should not pose the risk of injury if the runner continues to slowly increase their running distance and follow good running technique, hydration, electrolyte supplementation and stretching.

2. IT or iliotibial band injuries can be induced by a change in running shoes, surfaces or distances.
3. The optimal post run glycogen replacement is ½ grams of complex carbohydrates per pound within 15-30 minutes of exercise and should have a 4:1 carbohydrate to protein ratio. Chocolate milk is the perfect after exercise snack.

	Monday	Tuesday	Wednesday	Thursday	Friday	Saturday	Sunday
Date	8/3/09	8/4/09	8/5/09	8/6/09	8/7/09	8/8/09	8/9/09
Goal	Bike	Swim	Yoga	Run	Rest	Run with group	Rest
Duration	30 min	30 min	30 min	36 min		1:55	
Distance	?	?	NA	3 miles		10 miles	
AM pulse	---	---	---	---		---	
Weather	---	NA	Indoors	Slightly humid			
Temperature	Indoors	NA	NA	79°			
Time	12:05 pm	12:05 pm	7:10 pm	12:10 pm			
Terrain	---	NA	NA	Slight hills		Flat	
Run/Walk	---	NA	NA	3:1		3:1	
Rating	8	10	8	8		9	
Comments	It was hard to stay in the saddle.	I have no idea how far I swam…I just kept going!	Yoga & abs	Only slight right knee pain, stretched out really well	Hydrate prior to Saturday's run	No cramping	

Table 11-Training Log Week 11

Training Week 12

Sunday was a planned day of rest from exercise, but Bryan and I both overexerted ourselves at the National Whitewater Park in Charlotte, NC. The family and adventure rafting as well as the climbing wall weren't quite like running for miles, but it was exercise. If we had had more time, we would have amped it up even further with a bike ride or run on the trail at the facility, but unfortunately we had to get back to Apex at a reasonable hour to get the kids to bed and prepare for the week ahead. Although it was quick, the trip was a blast and an experience that I would recommend for anyone.

The following day, it was back to the humdrum of work as usual. My 12th week of training began with my normal lunch 3 mile run in downtown Durham. It was a typical North Carolina August day with highs in the 80s and extreme humidity. I was not worried about being able to do my run, but I acted wisely with a slower pace, 3:1 run/walk ratio, no tunes and lots of water. Ultimately, it was a great and energizing 36 minute run.

Per usual, it was hard to drag myself to the gym on Tuesday, but I did so anyway. Once in the pool, however, my body took control of my mind and I found myself swimming back and forth in the pool with ease. When my body started to fatigue, my mind kicked in again and reminded me that I was a woman that could run for 3 ½ hours; thus I could continue swimming beyond 10 minutes. Before I knew it, I swam 26 laps (650 yards or 0.37 miles) in 15 minutes. That was the longest continuous swim yet and it felt great! I could have and should have kept going, but I stopped more so in shock of my accomplishment instead of fatigue. Later that evening at home, my mind was filled with thoughts of another triathlon attempt in the future. I compared the distances of a Sprint, Olympic and Half Iron Man triathlon and found them to be 0.47, 0.93 and 1.2 miles, respectively. Maybe in the future I would do another Sprint triathlon and try to better my previous time or possibly pursue an Olympic triathlon.

That Wednesday, I was eager to complete my half day at work and return home to begin packing for the beach. My intent was to get enough packing done to squeeze in a session of yoga, but that didn't happen. Thus, the following day, I was determined to get in a run. Per usual, I did my typical 3 mile downtown Durham loop in the humid 80 degree weather. I then raced back to complete my day at work so that I could get home, finish packing and leave for the beach. That part of the day went well and we did get on the road to head for the beach, but 1.5 hours into the trip, I realized that I had left the key to the beach house at home. After looking at the predicted weekend weather report, which we should have done before we left, we realized that the Meteorologists were predicting rain for most of the weekend. Thus, we opted to return home and stay at home. That was a first, but the decision to return home was remarkably unchallenged by all.

To make up for not going to the beach, we headed west to Emerald Point in Greensboro on Friday that week. Harrison was just barely 45 inches tall and thus able to ride most of the slides. We had a blast going down slide after slide. We were all so relaxed and everyone had a great day. On the way home, the kids commented that they had the best day ever! In my mind, that was better than the usual trip to the beach. The only downside to that day, however, was that I was not able to really focus on hydrating well throughout the day. Thus, I did not feel well prepared for my first 18 mile run the following day.

That Saturday, I both eagerly and cautiously awaited my run with the Galloway training group. I looked forward to pushing myself to the new distance of 18 miles, but feared a reoccurrence of my knee pain and/or cramping. I had planned to get at least

8 hours of sleep the night before the run, but my husband and I happened to stay up until 11:30 watching a movie. With only 6 hours of sleep and poor pre-hydration the previous day, I arose from bed to drive towards the Saturday run site. Since we were supposed to be at the beach that weekend, Kristen was surprised to see me in Raleigh. I explained to her the mishaps of our trip during the first few miles of the run. We then continued our typical chit chat for many more miles. I felt really good throughout the first half of the run and experienced little to no knee pain or cramping. I dosed my typical Shot Blocks at mile 4 and GU at mile 8. I tried the vanilla and chocolate GU for the first time and it seemed like I was having an ice cream surprise while running. I also nibbled on 6 fat-free Fig Newtons throughout the run.

At the 10 mile mark, the group of us needing to complete 18 miles stopped at a McDonalds for a quick potty break and then headed out to complete the run. Close to the 14th mile, I began having a slight cramping sensation in the right thigh, but that did not limit me in any way. Many of us were rejuvenated at the 16th mile by orange slices, bananas, and candy bars that other members of our running group had put out for us. I thought the orange slices were the best that I had ever had. I purposefully avoided the chocolate, however, for fear of what it might do to my stomach.

The run progressed as normal for me until the17.5 mile mark. Within minutes, my minimal cramp in the right thigh progressed to a fully involved quadriceps cramp. Even though I could see the end of running course, I physically could not will my body to run. I could barely even walk. With each successive step, the cramp urged my body to remain still. Once finally able to walk to the end of the running path, I begin my stretching regime. Unfortunately, even that hurt. I spend a good 15 minutes alternating walking, stretching and standing still in order to get my body to move only 100 yards. Frustration swelled my thoughts. I knew that eventually the pain would pass, just as it had after the last long run, but I again feared that I would not be able to progress in training.

When I walked into the running store sponsoring the run for that week, the owner could see that I was visibly in pain and favoring my right side. He asked what was wrong and I gave him a brief summary of my cramping woes. I told him that I have always been prone to sweating profusely during exercise. He then recommended that I begin taking Hammer Enduralyte capsules for electrolyte replacement. He suggested that I take 2 capsules before initiating a long, hot run and continue taking 1 capsule each hour of progressive exercise. I hated the idea of having to take a pill for anything, but I never wanted to have that cramping pain again; thus, I was willing to try anything! In hindsight, I should have hydrated better and stretched more the day before the long run. Thus, my plan for the following run was to assure good stretching throughout the week, pre-hydrate to the best of my ability, hydrate well during the long run, and use the electrolyte capsules as directed.

The following morning was supposed to be a scheduled day of rest, but I felt compelled to do yoga. I was so stiff that I needed to do something to mobilize my body. The yoga session felt great and really helped. I then did my typical IT band stretching exercises and took an 800 mg Ibuprofen. I was sluggish throughout the rest of the day, but not in pain.

Key points this week:

1. It is imperative to hydrate well the day before a long run to reduce the incidence of dehydration and cramping during the run.
2. Those who sweat a lot while exercising or plan to exercise for an extended amount of time can benefit from the use of an electrolyte capsule supplement before and during exercise.
3. A gentle yoga or Pilates session helps to reduce cramping experienced the day after a hard and strenuous workout.

	Monday	Tuesday	Wednesday	Thursday	Friday	Saturday	Sunday
Date	8/10/09	8/11/09	8/12/09	8/13/09	8/14/09	8/15/09	8/16/09
Goal	Run	Swim	Too busy for exercise	Run	Rest	Run with group	Yoga
Duration	36 min	?		36 min		4:00	60 min
Distance	3 miles	?		3 miles		18 miles	NA
AM pulse	---	---		---		---	---
Weather	Humid	NA		Hot		Shade with occasional sun	NA
Temperature	80's	NA		80's		80's	NA
Time	12:00 pm	12:00 pm		12:10 pm		7:00 am	7:00 am
Terrain	Slight hills	NA		Slight hills		Flat	NA
Run/Walk	3:1	NA		3:1		3:1	NA
Rating	9	10		8		7	8
Comments	Great run even with the humidity	650 yards in 15 minutes-felt great!		We cancelled our beach trip since I forgot the key to the beach house.		Cramp at 17.5 miles-should have stretched more!	Felt compelled to do Yoga-stretching felt great.

Table 12-Training Log Week 12

TRAINING WEEK 13

The Jeff Galloway training journal quote for this week was absolutely perfect – "Each time you push through a discomfort barrier you make it easier to do it next time (Galloway, 1998, p 46)." Now doesn't that just summarize my experiences on the previous long runs! Maybe that quote was put at that particular part of the training journal because many of us begin to experience various ailments at this point in the training program. Maybe those words were meant specifically for novices like me. Regardless of my physical woes, however, I realize that I am getting physically stronger and that mentally I will be able to complete a full marathon. I also realize that my body has been pushed to its limits in the last 3 months and has weathered a lot of change. I just hope that I am not pushing myself too fast and thus risking injury.

On Monday, August 17th, I started my week with a typical 3 mile run at work. It was a hot and humid August day, but I was able to complete the run in 36 minutes. During the run, I waved to a few patients as I passed them on the downtown streets. I even overheard one saying to a co-worker, "there goes Stephanie running again." I am always glad when my patients see me running and working hard to stay fit. At least they know that I practice what I preach. During the later stages of the run, I reflected on how it is getting easier to run during the hotter weather. I don't particularly feel that I am running well; I just feel that I am running smarter with improved hydration, reduced pace and reduced physical exertion. Knowing that we would have a fancier meal that weekend without the kids, Bryan and I celebrated our 13th year of marriage that evening with a family meal at Panera. I don't really feel old enough to say that I have been married 13 years, but I am fortunate to say that it is the truth.

That Tuesday started and ended in chaos. My computer was down until11:30; thus, throughout the morning, I was doing my work but unable to complete my work. Once the system was up and running, I worked through lunch to catch-up and therefore had to skip my typical Tuesday swim. Instead of exercising that evening, I attended a Galloway arranged program with a Nutritionist to discuss how to eat well while preparing for long runs. Toward that end of the class, I asked the Nutritionist and attendants for their advice regarding my cramping on long runs. One peer recommended eating 6-8 bananas on the day of a long run since that is how he maintained his potassium levels while playing college football. I had no desire to follow his approach. A female peer stated her similar issues with Gatorade and stomach cramping/diarrhea and recommended the Hammer electrolyte replacement powder in place of Gatorade during the long runs. She was especially fond of the Hammer perpetuem product. She discussed that Gatorade and G2 are made with high fructose corn syrup and that is why they often lead to GI upset; Hammer products, on the other hand, do not contain fructose and arc thus often better tolerated. Furthermore, she supported and also utilized the electrolyte capsules that I had purchased at the running store after the 18 mile run. After speaking with her, I felt more secure with using the electrolyte capsules for longer runs and decided to purchase some Hammer electrolyte replacement powder.

The following day, I opted to swim for my midday workout. I entered the pool feeling great and energetic. I swam 400 yards in the pool, dumped the water out of my goggles, and swam an additional 225 yards. On the final lap, I felt so good that I decided to sprint as quickly as I could to the wall. Midway, however, I started cramping in my right foot and toes. At first, I feared that my body was betraying me. That fear, however, quickly turned into strength. I became determined to do just about anything and everything to avoid another exercise induced cramp. That evening, I went to an athletic store and purchased a huge container of the Hammer electrolyte replacement powder. Following the advice of the store attendant, I did not purchase the perpetuem brand. He warned that the protein in the perpetuem powder often started to break down and taste bad once heated by the sun. Though I was willing to try anything, I figured I would start with the product with the better taste.

That evening, I put a heaping teaspoon of the Hammer mandarin orange electrolyte replacement powder in 24 oz of water. I sipped on the "beverage" throughout the evening. I was pleased with the subtle orange flavor and no GI side effects. I felt that I was likely still behind on my electrolytes from the previous week's long run; thus I repeated the use of 1 heaping teaspoon full of the product in 32 oz of water the following day. During my lunch hour that Thursday, I did my typical 3 mile downtown Durham run and experienced minimal cramping. That evening, I commented to my husband about how much better I felt having used the powder. I finally felt like I was back to my normal, energetic self. Whether it was a placebo effect or not, I felt so much better!

The following day, I attended another medical education class. During the class, I sipped on 32 oz of water supplemented with a heaping teaspoon full of electrolyte powder. This time, I was not trying to replace electrolytes; instead, I was trying to get ahead in my electrolytes for my upcoming 10 mile run the following day. I hoped to get a good night's sleep to further prepare for the next day's run, but having a husband and 2 kids in my bed slightly hindered that goal. Upon awakening Saturday morning, I was a little sluggish, but overall I was ready to go. I purposefully took 2 electrolyte capsules and an 800 mg Ibuprofen with my typical pre-run breakfast of a Nutra-grain bar and a banana. During the walking breaks throughout the run, I alternated sips of water and Hammer electrolyte fluid. I followed my previous regime of 3

Shot Block gummies at 4 miles and a GU at 8 miles. One hour into the run, I took a third electrolyte capsule. I experienced slight pain in my right knee around the 4th and 7th mile and noticed a slight cramping sensation in the right quadriceps throughout the later half of the run; however, I finished the full 11 miles in an upright position and with a smile on my face. I did not experience a major cramp! I quickly stretched, grabbed some Galloway provided grub, and drove to see the last half of Harrison's first soccer game. As I watched the game without pain, I was able to thoroughly enjoy Harrison scoring his first soccer goal. Thank goodness…the extra electrolytes seemed to work!

Key points this week:

"Each time you push through a discomfort barrier you make it easier to do it the next time (Galloway, 2009. p 46)."

Gatorade can often cause gastrointestinal upset since it contains high fructose corn syrup that is harder for the body to digest. G2 is sweetened with high fructose corn syrup as well, but has less than its predecessor. Those with sensitive stomachs may do better with an electrolyte replacement fluid that is not made with fructose, such as a Hammer or Cytomel product.

If you know that you will be running more than 10 miles on a hot day, consider pre-hydrating the day before with an electrolyte substance prior to the run.

	Monday	Tuesday	Wednesday	Thursday	Friday	Saturday	Sunday
Date	8/17/09	8/18/09	8/19/09	8/20/09	8/21/09	8/22/09	8/23/09
Goal	Run	Unable to exercise	Swim	Run	Rest	Run with group	Rest
Duration	36 min		30 min	34 min		2:04	
Distance	3 miles		1250 yards	3 miles		11 miles	
AM pulse	---		---	---		---	
Weather	Hot & humid		NA	Humid		Humid	
Temperature	80's		NA	80's			
Time	12:10 pm		12:00 pm	12:00 pm		6:30 am	
Terrain	Slight hills		NA	Slight hills		Flat	
Run/Walk	3:1		NA	3:1		3:1	
Rating	8		10	9		8	
Comments	13 year wedding anniversary	Class on nutrition	Could have swum longer	Purposefully set a slower pace		Slight cramping	

Table 13-Training Log Week 13

Training Week 14

My 14th week of training was definitely different both professionally and personally. Haley and Harrison were away spending the whole week with Grandma and Grandpa. This was to be the first time that Bryan and I would be without kids while staying at home following our typical daily routines. Previously, when the kids were away at one of the grandparent's homes, Bryan and I would go on a short vacation and thus busy with new locations and experiences. With the kids away, it was extremely odd to go to work and return home not having to pick either of them up at daycare or school. It was strange not having to prepare a kid friendly meal in addition to an adult friendly meal. It was nice to go out to a nice restaurant for dinner without the added expense of having to pay a sitter. Throughout the week, I not only tried to interact more with my husband, but I also tried to be sure to pamper myself.

I began my work week with my typical Monday lunch time run in downtown Durham. Though hot, humid and habitual, I completed the 3 mile run in 34 minutes. Though boring at times, I think that keeping my Monday exercise routine consistent helps to eliminate the "what am I going to do today" dilemma and enable me to reinitiate my weekly workout routine with ease.

The following day, chaos ensued at work with the start of the county-wide Health Risk Appraisal process. Basically, in 6 days spanning the next 2 weeks, our plan was to bring in as many of the Durham County Government employees as possible to have their height, weight, blood pressure, and fasting labs performed. The first day of the assessments was to be one of the busiest days of the assessments. That Tuesday was as busy as expected. After standing on my feet for a solid 6 hours, I did not think that I had the energy to go for a swim, but I headed to the YMCA anyway. I had a hard time concentrating on my strokes during the first 3 lengths of the pool and seriously thought about abandoning my workout, but then willed my body to keep going. Ultimately, I stopped thinking and just started swimming. Fortunately, each lap got progressively easier. I found myself relaxing into my strokes. I stopped counting my laps and just kept swimming through the water. Ultimately, I swam for a solid 25 minutes without stopping. That was by far the best swim ever! I felt so strong. I then went home and cleaned my house for 4 hours. To some of you, that may seem like torture, but to me it was bliss. I had the house completely to myself since the kids were gone and Bryan was at his evening class. I was able to clean awhile, sit down to watch a little Oprah, clean a little more, have a leisurely dinner and then clean some more. What a cathartic experience!

The next was busier than the previous day with completing health risk appraisals at work. Again I was on my feet the whole day and wiped out at the completion of the work day. Fortunately, I had already scheduled to indulge myself with a sports massage. I often overheard other Galloway runners talk about the benefits of a massage after a long run. My initial hope was that a massage could reduce the incidence of future cramping while running; however, at the forefront of my mind that day was having the massage improve my low back pain that ensued after standing on my feet all day. There were times when the therapist's deep tissue work on my back and right quadriceps muscles took my breath away, but overall, the massage hurt so good. I felt so much better at the end of the massage that I signed up for a monthly massage at a reduced fee to ensure that I continued having regular massages while training for my marathon. That evening, I purposefully avoided aggressive exercise; however, Bryan and I took the dog to a local park and walked 3 miles on a greenway. It was really nice to get a little exercise while simultaneously having an uninterrupted conversation with my husband.

That Thursday continued to be chaotic at work, thus after leaving work, I decided to escape from my normal habit and go for a run around the scenic and shady Lake Pine. I followed the recommended 3:1 walk/run ratio and ran with my water belt. My plan was to complete 2 full laps around the lake for a 4 mile run. I experienced a little stiffness in my right quadriceps muscle, but the tightness did not progress to a full blown cramp. The stiffness even resolved with stretching upon completing the run. Overall, I was both mentally and physically satisfied with that run. It was nice to stray from the norm and be able to run without time deadlines. Even with taking every walk break, I completed the run in 44 minutes; thus the pace during my time running was better than a 10 minute mile. Though unexpected, it was nice to know that I could walk/run and still closely approximate my previous run only pace.

The following day was a planned day of rest and hydration to prepare for the upcoming 20 mile run with the Galloway group on Saturday. It was also the day to meet Grandma and Grandpa to pick-up the kids. The quiet time without the kids was initially nice, but it ultimately became unnerving. I was eager to hear and hug the kids. I was ready to fall back into our normal hectic routines. On the trip to get the kids, I pre-hydrated with a heaping scoop of Hammer electrolyte powder in 24 oz of water. I figured that this had worked well the previous week and thus I must be on to something good. I was also sure to stretch prior to going to bed that Friday night.

I awoke Saturday morning feeling well rested and ready to go. Just prior to initiating the run, I took 2 electrolyte capsules and one 800 mg Ibuprofen as preventative maintenance. I was glad to see my typical Galloway running mates as well as my most trusted supporter, Bernard. He had decided to run with our group to better understand the walk/run concept. Later, he divulged that he also wanted to assess my running skills. In the early miles of the run, it began to gently rain. It was both fun and refreshing to run with a cool mist hitting our bodies. At 6 miles into the run, Bernard informed me that he was only going to run 10 of the planned 20 miles. I initially feared that our slower pace and scheduled walk breaks would bore him, but later realized that he was slightly struggling to keep going with the group. He then disclosed that, even though he was routinely running about 14 miles each weekend, those miles were accrued on a treadmill. He confessed that running on a treadmill is significantly different than running on the open road. I agreed whole heartedly.

I parted ways with Bernard and at least half of the running group at the 10 mile mark to head out for another 10 mile run around Shelley Lake and the surrounding area. We purposefully planned the second half of the run in a more shady area to minimize our physical exertion. I was sure to be consistent with taking an electrolyte capsule every hour, consuming 3 shots blocks or a GU packet every 4 miles, and alternating my intake of water and Hammer electrolyte fluid during at least every other walk break. I had no cramping or stiffness what so ever. I felt WONDERFUL at the completion of the 4 hour 20 minute run. The run was then concluded with an early lunch and good conversation with 2 running mates. That was, to date, the best run ever. Bryan was even amazed when I came home with a huge smile on my face. He had become accustomed to seeing me hobble into our home after long runs.

Later that day, we ventured to the community pool to capitalize on one of the last warm days of summer. While at the pool, I began talking to my neighbor. Lo and behold, she too is a member of the Galloway training group. Most recently, she has been running with the 11:00 pace group. I reflected on the fact that it is impossible to know everyone in our now 400+ training group, but found it reassuring that someone so close by might now become my running partner during the off season.

Key points this week:

1. Treadmill running is different than running on the open road. If you want to be prepared to run on the road, do most of your running outdoors.
2. Prehydrating with electrolyte powder the day prior to a long run, taking 2 electrolyte capsules before a long run and 1 capsule each hour during the run, supplementing with GU or Shot Blocks every 4 miles during the run, and alternating sips of water and an electrolyte drink every other walk break resolved my cramping during a long hot run. You will need to find what works best for you.

	Monday	Tuesday	Wednesday	Thursday	Friday	Saturday	Sunday
Date	8/24/09	8/25/09	8/26/09	8/27/09	8/28/09	8/29/09	8/30/09
Goal **Duration**	Run 34-36 min	Swim 30 min	Walk 1 hour	Run 44 min	Rest	Run with group 4:20	Rest
Distance	3 miles	?	3 miles	4 miles		20 miles	
AM pulse	---	---	---	---		---	
Weather	Hot & humid	NA	Nice	Hot & humid		Shady	
Temperature	80°	NA				Mid 70's	
Time	12:10 pm	2:00 pm	6:30 pm	2:00 pm		6:45 am	
Terrain	Slight hills	NA	Flat	Flat		Flat trail	
Run/Walk	3:1	NA	Walk only	3:1		3:1	
Rating	8	10	9	9		10	
Comments		I thought about abandoning workout, but had the best swim ever!	I had a wonderful, relaxing walk with Bryan.	I noticed stiffness & cramping, but it improved with stretching.	Hydrate	Best run ever!	

Table 14-Training Log Week 14

Training Week 15
Half Marathon

This week started just like many others with a 3 mile run in Downtown Durham during lunch. Feeling energetic due to a sudden cooling in the temperature to 70 degrees, I decided to run with my I-pod tunes and no walk break. It was so great to attack the run not fearing heat exhaustion or dehydration. I completed the run in 30 minutes and was satisfied that I could still run a 10 minute mile. At times, it is a little disheartening to run in the 10:30 pace group, but actually run at an 11:30-12:30 minute per mile pace. I understand the concept of running slower to adjust for temperature elevations and successful completion of longer mileage, but it still is somewhat of a killjoy to look at the time it takes to run the longer distances at a slower pace. Overall, that Monday run started off what was to become a very satisfying week of exercise.

The following day, I wasn't feeling as energetic as the previous day since we were entering the second week of the health risk appraisals with the Durham County Government employees. Though a little mentally fatigued, I set out for my typical Tuesday swim. The previous day, Haley had started a stoke clinic with her new swim team, the Marlins of Raleigh, and I was planning to implement some of the swim techniques that I heard the coaches reviewing with the swimmers. As I pulled the water under my body while swimming freestyle, I made sure to continue the stroke all the way back to the back surface of the water and somewhat flip the water off my hand. By rotating my arm a full 180 degrees during each stroke, I found that I was moving through the water much more efficiently and thus taking less strokes and breaths during each lap in the pool. It was also fun to get a little sassy with flipping the water off my hand at the completion of each stroke. Overall, I swam ½ mile (800 yards) in 25 minutes. I found an inner peace and sense of personal strength while in the water. That was yet another great workout!

The mid 70 degree weather continued that Wednesday. After picking up the kids early from daycare and school due to an early release day, we headed to a local park to enjoy the great outdoors. While the kids played with what seemed to be the majority of kids living in Apex, I walked the dog around the path surrounding the wooden play equipment. As I walked, I could see the kids running, climbing and chatting with their friends. After walking a good 2 miles, I took Ruffles into the play area to rest. Many of the kids came up to pet Sir Ruffles and ended up having wood chips kicked on them as my digger dog began attempting to dig to China. Imagine this…a white Westie digging in black dirt! That was a hoot! Later that evening, I did a session of Yoga. The instructor worked out areas that I didn't know that I had! I'll definitely tune her in again for a great workout.

Thursday brought on the completion of the health risk appraisal process and a sense of energy that I directed into my mid afternoon workout. After getting my flu shot at my doctor's office in less than 5 minutes, I found that I had 2 hours before I needed to pick-up the kids; thus, I donned my running attire and I-pod. The temperature had increased slightly into the 80s, but it was not as humid as previous weeks had been. I opted to run my typical Olive Chapel path. I didn't think that I had time to attempt a four mile course and tackle "the hill" even though I was running without any walking breaks. Ultimately, I was able to complete the 3 mile run in 34 minutes. It felt good to run an old, familiar path other than my downtown Durham County loop. That run left me feeling invigorated and ready to tackle my first half marathon.

That Friday, I worked until 12:30, went to the store to get a few essentials for our beach trip and headed home to begin packing. Of course the first items that I packed were my race supplies. I double and triple checked to be sure to have everything that I would need for the race. The following morning around 8 am, we dropped off the dog at the vet's office for boarding and begin our trip towards Virginia Beach. On the way, I consumed 32 oz of water mixed with a heaping spoonful of Hammer electrolyte powder. We arrived at our hotel around 2 pm, unloaded the van and drove to the convention center to pick-up my race packet. As I approached the counter to pick up my supplies, I admit that I was surprised by two things. First, I was surprised at the large number of people checking in at the slower race times such as my own. When I initially registered for the race, I estimated my finish time as 2 hours and 40 minutes; thus, I was to start the race in the back of the pack in corral 24. I knew that my plan was to complete the race at a quicker time, but I dared not change my corral number and potentially jinx myself. While checking in at the corral 24 booth, I was pleased to see many others checking in at both similar and slower paces. The other thing that surprised me during packet pick-up was the diversity of people checking in on the other side of the room in the faster pace groups. I was not trying to be judgmental, but some did not look physically fit enough to finish the race in their predicted time. I found myself wondering what they were thinking and if they would succeed in achieving their quicker race time. I found myself experiencing a sense of jealousy towards those that did appear very physically fit who were registering in the lower corral numbers. I wanted to be like them. Overall, comparing myself to others gave me a little more incentive to push harder to achieve my race time goal of 2 hours and 20 minutes. I wanted to successfully blow my predicted time away!

From the convention center, we walked 6 blocks to the beach to frolic and play in the sand and water. The water was freezing cold, but that didn't keep Haley from submerging herself and then asking us to take her deeper into the ocean. Fortunately, Bryan went out with Haley as I stayed closer to the shore with Harrison. He and I spent hours karate chopping and kicking the waves as they passed. So much for a day without exercise! Exhausted, we left the ocean front around 5:30 and sought out a place for dinner on the boardwalk. It was predetermined that we would go somewhere for pasta to allow me to fuel up for the next day's race. We happened upon an Italian restaurant named Giovanni's and were fortunate enough to go right to our seats. I opted for the spinach ravioli with a house salad, water, and 3 pieces of bread. As we left the restaurant about an hour later, we encountered a huge line of patrons waiting to enter. I presume that the line predominantly consisted of runners that were eagerly awaiting their pre-race carbohydrate load. Boy was I glad for small children that dictate having an early dinner.

Upon getting back to the hotel room around 7:00, Bryan went downstairs to get in a little study time knowing that I was soon to go to sleep with the kids. I began reading my race information while the kids watched a cartoon. I fastened my bib to the shirt that I was planning to wear the following day. I set out all of my race gear in the bathroom to reduce the potential of waking up anyone the following morning. Around 8 pm, the kids and I turned off all the lights and slipped under the bed covers to begin watching a movie. Periodically, I closed my eyes to visualize the race and take deep relaxing breaths. By 9:30, no one was really interested in the movie so I turned off the TV. I was amazed at how easily I fell asleep. I was even able to quickly fall back to sleep when Bryan returned from his studying.

I awoke independently at 4 am. I had planned to sleep until 5 am, but I feared that an abundance of people would be waiting for the hotel van and that my commute to the race site might be delayed. The previous day, I was told that the hotel van would shuttle us to a city bus and then the bus would take us to the staging area for the race. I was afraid that all of the transfers would not occur smoothly and thus I would get to the staging area late. Therefore, I hopped out of bed, dressed and entered the hotel lobby at 4:30 am. There were only about 15 runners waiting for the shuttle. I was able to get on the first shuttle leaving the hotel. In route, I ate my typical pre-race Nutra Grain breakfast bar and banana. I also took my 800 mg Ibuprofen and 2 electrolyte capsules. I was pleased to find out that the driver would be able to get us closer to starting line than expected since some of the roads on the boardwalk were not yet closed. I was so glad that I would not have to rely on yet another means of transportation to get to the starting line.

I arrived at the staging area at 5 am. I was surrounded by more port-a-johns than people. Every 15 minutes or so, an influx of approximately 50 people filled the convention center parking lot. At 5:30, I happened to spot a fellow Galloway team member, Jim. We passed the next hour with chat about our hotel accommodations, previous runs, future runs, and families. At 6am, we moved closer to the bus drop-off site in hopes of seeing other Galloway runners. By that time, the city buses were arriving two at a time every few minutes and unloading a multitude of runners. Quickly, the parking lot became standing room only.

At 6:30, I received a call from a fellow Galloway runner that he was trying to find me at the corral area. I then realized that I was not where I had said I would be at 6 am and thus used Rob's directions to get to the correct site. Within minutes of arriving at corral 24, Jim and I were greeted by Rob, Sandy, Dawn, and Kristen. I was SO GLAD to be reunited with members my running group. I knew that I would have comrades to help push me through the race. Prior to the beginning of the race, Jim decided to run with another Galloway runner at a slower pace with 2:1 run/walk cycles. The other five of us discussed trying to run a 10 minute mile pace while taking a one minute walking break every 3 minutes. Depending on our time, we would then begin running without walking at around the 10 mile mark. Hopefully we would all finish together at our goal time of 2 hours and 20 minutes.

Just before the beginning of the race, the National Anthem was sung by a young girl born the year of the first Virginia Beach half marathon. Her voice sounded older than her 8 years and she did an exceptional job belting out the high notes. I couldn't help but think about my daughter Haley, who is eagerly looked forward to turning 8 this year. Soon after the completion of the anthem, I heard the first horn blow. The race had begun! The five of us waited patiently for our turn to run. Sandy snapped a quick photo of the group on her new I-phone and quickly updated her Facebook account. She wrote, "Starting line. T minus 15 minutes." As we eagerly waited to begin, we all took note of the 4 red balls that kept circulating through the air in front of us as a runner juggled while waiting. We also made numerous comments about outrunning the man with the lobster hat that was just in front of us. At 7:39.08 am, the horn finally blew for us. After quick high fives, we started to run. For the first mile, it was hard to run at a specific pace since there were so many people. We were constantly weaving in an out of other runners. After the first mile, however, we were better able to set a consistent pace. We opted to run through the first walk break and follow Rob. He pushed us for the first few miles at an average pace of 9:30 minutes per mile. No wonder we were all demanding a walk break at the 11 minute mark! From then on, we purposefully stuck to the plan of running a 10 minute mile pace and taking each walking break. We reached the 5K marker 32:57 into the race. Honestly, I found the first 3 miles tiring. It was like I had to work out the stiffness and get my body going.

As we reached the 3.5 mile marker, we were passed by the elite runners who were running in the opposite direction. They were on their 9th mile and they were flying! I took note of their lean bodies and effortless strides. I was envious. I was then pleasantly distracted by a great reggae band. Their music continued playing in my head and got me through the next few miles. I then loaded up on 3 Shot Blocks and continued moving down the road. It was great to encounter a different band every few miles. My favorite group came close to the 10K marker at 1:05:55. The group was led by a teenage female rocking on the guitar to the song "Higher Ground." That song helped me run through the military base and the sunniest portion of the race. Soon thereafter, we came to a very congested water stop. Rob was lost in the crowd and never seen again. The four of us remaining had no choice but to keep moving. We continued running a 10 minute per mile pace with walk breaks every 3 minutes. Kristen began having stitches in her side, thus we slowed the pace down a little for one run session. After a few minutes, she was feeling better and we resumed our faster pace. Unfortunately, at 9 miles she opted to slow down her pace and told us to continue ahead. I thus took in a GU with an electrolyte capsule and kept moving with our now smaller group.

Dawn, Sandy and I reached the 10 mile mark at 1:47.10. I was feeling great and full of energy. I felt that each cheerleader infused me with positive acclamations and each band ignited my inner fire. I was ready to run without breaks, but my group was not. Sandy was starting to fatigue and requested to continue taking walking breaks until the 11th mile. Dawn and I acquiesced, knowing that pacing ourselves would ultimately enable us to finish stronger at the end. Once at the 11.4 mile marker at 2:01.56, Dawn and I were bursting with energy, wanting to run without stopping, and realizing that we still had the potential to make our goal time of 2:20. Sandy, however, felt that she needed to continue running with walking breaks. Our now group of 3 was once again reduced.

When Dawn and I got closer to the boardwalk, the crowds became larger and louder. As we rounded 14th Street onto Atlantic Avenue, I fed off the energy of the crowd and significantly picked up my pace. I didn't have a Garmin to determine my exact pace, but I could extrapolate from previous training that I was well under a 10 minute mile. It was great to be passing people and not getting passed. I felt I was peaking, not pooping out. It was wonderful! My sense of wellbeing was somewhat diminished when I felt my tampon fall out in the middle of the run. I had never had that happen before and it took me a few steps to realize that there was nothing that I could do but keep running. When I saw the 12.3 mile marker at 2:10.55, I had yet another slight sinking sensation in the pit of my stomach. I thought I was a little further in the race than my actual distance. I did not know if I would be able to keep up my stamina up, but I knew that I had to maintain the same pace to finish at 2:20. I took another GU for a burst of electrolytes and caffeine. Soon after the thought of fatigue hit my mind, Dawn stated that she did not know if she could continue running without walking. At that moment, something within me took over. I told her that she could not stop because we were going to finish the race together. She didn't know that I too was feeling the burden of our previous 12+ miles. I would have walked had she walked. Fortunately, she succumbed to my demands and kept running at our previous pace. She thinks that I kept her running, but in truth, she is why I keep running.

As we made the final turn onto the boardwalk, I had yet another surge of energy. Having reviewed the course map prior to the race, I knew that I had less than a mile to go. Even though I had only done one magic mile in training, I kept telling myself that this was my magic mile time. I had to keep pushing. It would all end soon and I had all day to lick any wounds. I had to leave it all out there on the course and I knew that I was so close to my 2:20 goal. My feet kept turning over one after the other. I yearned for the finish line. I continued to push forward with Dawn by my side. Ultimately, we finished the half marathon at 2:17.10. I was so proud of myself. I had no significant pain throughout the race. Sure, my feet and toes felt used and abused, but I finished in an upright posture with what was likely a huge smile on my face. Dawn and I shared a hug to celebrate our success and then continued walking down the boardwalk with the crowd. I downed a full bottle of water and followed that quickly with a lot of Cytomel. We then approached the station with the finisher's medals. As the man handed me the medal, I couldn't wait to put it around my neck. I was surprised by it's heaviness as it hit my sweaty chest, but proud to feel its weight.

As soon as I got the medal, my thoughts quickly turned to my family. I so wanted to share this moment with them. I thus called Bryan with my cell. Once on the line, he immediately said, "Way to go baby." He had been receiving text messages throughout the race documenting my progress. He had just received a text that I had finished the race. He knew that I had bettered my goal time. As I waited at the ferris wheel to be reunited with him and the kids, I was pleased to see Sandy and then Kristen. Sandy finished just under the 2:20 time and Kristen finished at 2:24. I was relieved to know that they finished with such a good time and impressed that they had done so on their own.

When Bryan, Haley and Harrison arrived, we shared hugs and kisses. The kids quickly informed me that they were starving and needing food. I introduced Bryan to my fellow Galloway runners and he snapped a few post race photos. I then crossed a gate to leave the race area. Even though I had gotten a special yellow armband at the Expo and had every intention of having a cold beer to celebrate the completion of the race, I left the race course without having a beer. Once in the bathroom, I was shocked to not see my feminine hygiene product in my running shorts. Oh my gosh…where did it go? Did it fall out on the race path? Did someone see it? These are all questions that entered my mind. I contemplated not including this highly embarrassing moment in this book, but I felt it necessary to share my experience and warn others of the need for larger feminine hygiene products while running. Hopefully, with the sharing of this information, this situation would not happen to anyone else.

Knowing that the crowd and noise were just a little too much for the kids, we stopped at an ice cream shop on the boardwalk for dipped cones and then made our way to our car. Bryan thought it would be nice to take the kids to a local park until the crowds at the beach dissipated. We spent the next few hours at "Mount

Trashmore" which is a park close to downtown Virginia Beach that is built on a previous landfill. The kids had fun climbing, swinging, and rolling down the HUGE hills. We then ventured to Subway for a quick lunch before heading to the beach for more excitement. The crowds had definitely improved by the time we made it back to the boardwalk, but the beach was still packed with people. Bryan again went out in the water with Haley and I opted to stay on the shore with Harrison. This time, however, I let him fight the waves as I sat on a beach towel watching. I was definitely tired and sensing the need to preserve my energy.

Later that evening, I was tired but not exhausted. I was sure to take an additional Ibuprofen with dinner and stretch before bed, but my previous cramping woes seemed a distant memory. I was glad that I was not like the man I saw being carried across the finish line held upright with the support of a women and man. He appeared white as a sheet and limp as a noodle. Later, I was stunned to find out that a 23 year old died on the boardwalk at a medic station during the race. According to his friend's comments in the paper, he was in good health and had trained well prior to the race. I reminded myself that running 13.1 miles is not an easy feat. His death helped me to again realize the importance of good preparation, hydration, and pacing during longer runs. I will never run another race without reflecting on the frailty of human life.

Key points this week:

1. If running any race at Virginia Beach, I recommend paying the extra money to stay on the beach and close to the race venue. It will save a lot of time commuting, a lot of money in parking fees and help one stay better focused on why they are there…to run a race.
2. It is imperative to have a mental footprint of the race course, water stations, rescue stations, and mile markers prior to the race. These serve as mental cues to keep you moving toward the ultimate goal…the finish line.

3. Women, use larger feminine hygiene products when running.
4. I realized that I push myself harder when I am pushing others. I am only as strong as my strongest group member.
5. Pay close attention to your body throughout a race. How are you breathing? What is your heart rate? What is your perceived effort level? Keep in mind that healthy people have died attempting similar goals. If your body is telling you to stop, please stop.

	Monday	Tuesday	Wednesday	Thursday	Friday	Saturday	Sunday
Date	8/31/09	9/1/09	9/2/09	9/3/09	9/4/09	9/5/09	9/6/09
Goal	Run	Swim	Yoga	Run	Rest	Rest	Race
Duration	30-36 min	30 min	42 min	34 min			2:17.10
Distance	3 miles	½ mile or 960 yards	NA	3 miles			13.1 miles
AM pulse	---	---	---	---			---
Weather	Nice!	NA	NA				Sunny, no humidity
Temperature	70's	NA	NA	80's			74°
Time	12:10 pm	2:00 pm		2:00 pm			7:30 am
Terrain	Slight hills	NA	NA	Slight hills			Flat
Run/Walk	Run only	NA	NA	Run only			3:1
Rating	10	10	10	9			10
Comments	Energetic!	Felt strong!				Drive to Virginia Beach	Virginia Beach ½ Marathon

Table 15-Training Log Week 15

TRAINING WEEK 16

I entered my 16th week on training on a high from my accomplishments during my first half marathon. I took the obligatory day off from strenuous exercise on Monday. On Tuesday, however, I was eager to exercise. Just prior to entering the pool, I purposefully took a few deep breaths to calm myself down. I then swam continuously for 20 minutes and covered 800 yards in the pool. I worked on fully extending my arms to gain better distance with each pull through the water. Overall, it was a very good and satisfying swim.

That evening, I went to purchase a new pair of running shoes. Since beginning the Galloway program 3 months ago, I had put about 300 miles on my running shoes. On average, running shoe replacement is recommended after 350-550 miles, but those running more than 25 miles a week should consider changing their shoes every 3-4 months. Furthermore, runners that are heavier may find it necessary to change their shoes closer to the 350 mileage whereas lighter runners may opt for replacement at the later mileage. Though I did not meet any of the above criteria, I felt that my old shoes were no longer giving me the same bounce as before. I opted to get the same type of running shoe, but due to supply issues, I had to buy a 10 wide instead of 10 regular. I hoped to avoid negative consequences by making as little change as possible in the type of shoe used.

My plan for Wednesday was to do some form of exercise after work, but after having a very relaxing massage, I was no longer good for anything. Thus, I succumbed to being lazy. The following day, I was very busy at work. I should have worked through lunch, but I knew that I needed to get in my second run of the week. Since it was a cooler day and I was in somewhat of a time crunch, I decided to run without walk breaks and listen to my I-pod. Since it was my 36th birthday, I found myself reflecting on my age and current health status throughout the run. I am so much healthier than 4 years ago. I remembered when running one mile was exhausting. Two and a half miles into the run, I had enough energy left to sprint to the end of my 3 mile run. Overall, the run felt very good. Upon returning to work, I felt more productive. Once at home, I opened my birthday package. Bryan and the kids had bought me a pair of biking shoes. Now I would have the opportunity to get use to clipping in while spinning. In my mind, it was the next logical step towards progressing to cycling on the open road at some point in the future.

Friday was a typical day without exercise. I was sure to hydrate well with electrolyte replacement powder and water. I was also sure to stretch before going to bed. I wanted to be as rested and prepared as possible for the 23 mile group run planned for the next day. Per usual, however, I got to bed much later than expected. Upon awakening at 5:30 on Saturday morning, I seriously contemplated going back to bed. I did not, however, since I knew that I was not mentally prepared to run 23 miles by myself. Sluggishly, I got dressed, grabbed my breakfast and running gear, and drove to the group meeting site. I arrived at the Art Museum parking lot in the dark and half awake. As I waited for the group to arrive, I took my 2 electrolyte capsules and one 800 mg Ibuprofen. I knew that both would be needed to enable me to complete such a long run.

We began the run in the darkness of the early morning. Ron ran with us to assure that we ran a slower pace and stayed together as a group. He counseled us that on a long run over 20 miles, the first 10 miles are just a warm-up and should thus be taken very slow and easy. Never before did I think that I would consider 10 miles a warm-up! After about 2 hours, we completed the first portion of the day's run. I was happy to complete the first 10 miles somewhat effortlessly and feeling strong. After taking a "hard stop" for everyone to use the bathroom and fill up their water/electrolyte bottles, we set out for the second 10 mile run. We took a slightly different route but still ran predominantly around Shelley Lake. Ron often shouted out reminders to hydrate and supplement with electrolytes. I did my best to adhere to my every 4 mile supplementation regime. From about the 12th to the 14th mile, Cara had us playing a name game. One person would say the first and last name of a famous person and the next person had to think of another famous person whose first name started with the first letter of the previous person's last name. For example, Cara said Mel Gibson and the next person said Gary Coleman. This game was very successful in helping to pass time and take our mind off of the thought of fatigue. It also helped us get to know one another better. The lone guy playing the game with us was obviously into sports since all of the names he spoke were of famous athletes. All of us agreed that we wanted to go to Michelle's house to listen to music since she always seemed to spout the name of a wonder musician. Others were apparently well versed in literature since they often spoke the names of great authors. My mind was in a child's word given that our TV is often playing children's programming. Two of my famous actors were Strawberry Shortcake and Fred Flintstone. No matter what, my kids are always with me. Even though I found the name game a welcomed distraction, it may have been too distracting. I failed to pay attention to our distance while playing the game and ultimately took my GU and electrolyte supplement later than normal. Though it did not affect me at the time, I think it contributed to my fatigue at a later mile.

On mile 18 or so, we ascending a large hill and I found myself feeling pretty winded. Fortunately, I knew that the course was going to be flat for the remainder of the run and that I was no more than 3 minutes away from a walk break. Those realizations gave me the ability to keep running. By the end of the 20th mile, I had recuperated and was ready to head out for the final 3 miles to complete the 23 mile run.

Only four of us set out for the additional 3 miles. Since Sandy had not been feeling well the previous night, her plan was to walk the majority of the final miles. Another runner chose to stay with Sandy to assure that she pulled through without problem. Missy and I were the only two remaining who planned to continue our traditional walk/ run ratio and pace to complete the 23 mile run. The first 1.5 miles were easy with intermittent conversation and a slightly faster pace that our previous 20 miles. Missy had a Garmin to track our pace, but I never asked exactly how fast we were running. Truthfully, at that point, I didn't care. During the final1.5 miles of the run, I began to experience a cramping sensation in my right thigh. Of course, all of my ailments of the past came to mind. I recalled that I had only taken 3 electrolyte capsules throughout the run. Now 5 hours into the run, I should have taken at least 5 capsules. I also knew that I had not drunk as much water as normal. During the next 2 walk breaks, the cramping sensation worsened. I verbalized to Missy that I needed to continue running to attempt to ward-off increased cramping. She was willing to try to run out the last mile or so with me. Thus, when my Gym-Boss beeped for us to walk, we continued running. After the next three minute interval, it was somewhat distressful to hear the signal to walk. I needed and wanted to walk, but I feared bigger consequences from walking than running. After running through at least 4 Gym-Boss cycles, we did finally stop for a walk. Fortunately, the cramping had subsided some and walking did not lead to increased cramping. At the next signal to run, both Missy and I were slow to initiate the run. Missy commended on how taking the walking breaks really do make a difference. That last ¼ mile seemed to never end. I honestly wondered if my legs were going to let me finish the run. I was so glad to finally reach our end point. I was then shocked to find out that we had ran a total of 23.25 miles instead of just 23 miles. What an accomplishment and what overachievers!

Missy and I then walked about 300 yards to our cars. After sharing a hug to congratulate one another, we parted ways. I then spent the next 10 minutes stretching, walking around and drinking more fluids. Once driving toward home, I took a detour to purchase my typical post-run bagel and chocolate milk. After standing in line for a few minutes inside the cold bagel shop, I felt compelled to stretch my legs. With sweat soaked hair and clothing, I did a few upright stretches. I noticed a few odd looks, but I didn't care. I had to stretch. Twenty minutes later, I was at home and again stretching. Only then did I really feel that cramp fully resolve. I had planned to soak in a cold bath, but ended-up filling up the bath tub with lukewarm water. I took it as a sign to avoid a freezing cold bath. Minutes later, I was prone on the couch and swallowing down a second 800 mg Ibuprofen for the day. My legs felt heavy. I remembered hearing another runner talk about reducing post run leg swelling by putting her legs "up a wall" after running a long distance. Thus, I laid on the hardwood floor in our family room with my legs fully extended up the wall. It felt good to feel the heaviness leaving my tired legs. I would have preferred to lay there for a long time, but Bryan was ready to get on with our previously made plans to go to the Museum of Life and Science in Durham. They were having a special day featuring the Star Wars characters. We knew that would fascinate Harrison. Somewhat reluctantly, I moved to the van. We walked around at the museum for about 2 hours and then had a nice family dinner. At 8:30 am, I was spent. As soon as the kids were in bed, I too went to bed. My body needed sleep.

The following morning, I awoke feeling stiff. I immediately ate breakfast and took an 800 mg Ibuprofen. I had no plans for any form of exercise that day, but I ended-up mowing the grass. I thought that doing some easy exercise would help me work off the lactic acid in my muscles. Plus, the grass needed to be cut and there was not a goat to be found. After mowing the grass, I continued feeling achy and stiff. Thus, I spent the rest of the day watching TV and only doing what had to be done.

Key points this week:

1. Running shoes should be changed every 350-550 miles or every 3-4 months if running over 25 miles a week. Some, however, feel the need to replace their shoes more often.
2. Buying shoes a half size larger or in a wider size may prevent damage to the toenails that can result from running frequently or longer distances.
3. It is imperative to strictly follow a plan for water and electrolyte supplementation during long runs in order to keep the body working at its optimum potential.
4. Elevating the legs above the heart after a long run helps to promote venous return to the heart and thus reduce swelling of the lower extremities after a long run. Simply put, it really helps those tired, heavy legs feel better.

	Monday	Tuesday	Wednesday	Thursday	Friday	Saturday	Sunday
Date	9/7/09	9/8/09	9/9/09	9/10/09	9/11/09	9/12/09	9/13/09
Goal	Rest	Swim	No exercise	Run	Rest	Run with group	Rest
Duration		30 min		35 min		? 5 hours	
Distance		?700 yards		3 miles		23 miles	
AM pulse		---		---		---	
Weather		NA					
Temperature		NA		High 70's			
Time		12:00 pm		12:00 pm		6:30 am	
Terrain		NA		Slight hills		Flat	
Run/Walk		NA		Run only		3:1	
Rating		8		8			
Comments			Relaxing Massage		New shoes	Slow and easy, no cramping	

Table 16-Training Log Week 16

Training Week 17

On Monday, I planned to slip back into my normal workout pattern. I set out to run my typical 3 mile Durham County loop at lunch; however, this run was not the norm. I started the run still feeling stiff from my 23 mile run over the weekend. I thought that running would help to work out some of the stiffness. Boy was I wrong! I began running on that hot, but not humid, 88 degree day knowing that I needed to take every walk break. The first mile felt fine, but I began feeling stiff during the second mile. Given my normal determination, I continued to push myself. By the third mile, I was exhausted. I willed my body to keep going to complete the full three miles. Upon getting back to the office, I ran into Bernard and commented about how awful I felt during the run. He chastised me for running so soon after a 23 mile run.

The following day, I both mentally and physically did not want to swim but again my stubbornness drove me to the gym. After only 150 yards, I switched from freestyle to backstroke to preserve my energy. I felt like a limp noodle in the water. I ultimately swam for a full 25 minutes, but the workout was yet another physical toll on my body. While showering after the swim, I finally acknowledged to myself that I was physically tired and thus needed to rest. I also came to the realization that had I been monitoring my resting heart rate each morning as recommended by Jeff Galloway, I likely would have noticed an increase in my heart rate indicative of fatigue. That too would have helped clue me into the need for more rest. In hindsight, I should have had a very light workout such as walking or yoga or considered taking a second consecutive day for rest and recuperation after running 23 miles. I pushed myself too hard and too soon.

In hopes of resting but gaining core strength and flexibility, I did 40 minutes of yoga that Wednesday. I purposefully exercised while the kids were at school so that I could really focus on the breathing and relaxing aspect of yoga. Plus, I needed some "me" time. Ultimately, that workout helped to rejuvenate my body. In the future, I will likely do a nonaggressive yoga session on the second day following any run over 20 miles.

I planned to do my second run of the week on Thursday. I was a little concerned that I would again be pushing myself too soon, but I was feeling much better than earlier in the week. Since it was raining outside and I had to look fresh for work after the run, I opted to go to the gym to run on a treadmill during lunch. I set the MPH for 6.0, fired-up my I-Pod and began running. The pace and constant running were not a problem, they were actually easier than I recalled. The boredom, however, was tremendous. I will admit that at times I get bored while running the same old outside paths week after week, but running on a treadmill is so monotonous! I vowed to myself to only run on a treadmill in the future if there are no other feasible running options.

That Friday, I took a day off from exercise to rest. I did, however, sufficiently carb load for my Saturday run by eating a wonderful pasta dish and cheesecake from the Cheesecake Factory. Mmmm...so good! Thank goodness the meal was at lunch instead of dinner. I may have not been able to get out of bed for Saturday's run had I eaten that much food for dinner.

All week long, I was both looking forward to and dreading our Saturday run. Since the second half of my first marathon would take place in Umstead Park, I looked forward to running the course and committing its layout to memory. I knew that the experience would prove useful during the marathon. My fear of the run, however, stemmed from comments from many people about how deceiving and hard the hills in Umstead Park can be. Even though we only planned to do a 10 mile run, I was afraid that I would find the hills overwhelming. As our somewhat smaller group started the run, we eased into our typical pace. I felt good. The right quadriceps pain that had once ailed me was far from my mind. As we made our way into Umstead Park, I found the shade and scenery of the trees refreshing. I also found the sandy path more forgiving on my joints. As we approached the first incline, I couldn't help but wonder if we had already began our interaction with one of Umstead's notoriously bad hills. The first incline was not that bad, but the second hill lived up to the path's reputation.

As we approached another hill at about 1.5 miles into the run, all of the most experienced runners commented that this hill would seem to go on forever. They encouraged us all to pace ourselves. Ron went to the front of the group to lead our climb. As we ascended, we winded from the right to the left. I again wondered if I had made a poor choice for my first marathon. Seven minutes or two runs and one walk break later, we finally made it to the top of the hill. Then, we enjoyed a long descent down the hill. Boy, I was glad when that one was over. The next substantial hill came at approximately 3.5 miles into the run. As we ran that hill, Kelli told me that they call it the graveyard hill since there is an old graveyard at the top of the hill. Believe me, I was so glad to see that graveyard! We then continued past a clearing in which you are able to see a glimpse of the Raleigh International Airport. The remainder of the initial 5.5 miles was relatively benign compared to the initial stages of the run, although, I knew that we would again face significant uphill climbs before completing the run.

Close to the 7.5 mile mark, we began our ascent up the backside of the second steep hill. I was able to mentally push myself up the hill knowing that a long and winding descent followed by flat surfaces was only steps away. At the peak of the hill, both my running mates and I were slightly out of breath and thus very quiet. Within minutes, however, everyone rebounded back and the uttering of conversations resumed. I talked to Ron about my thoughts for future training next year. I stated that my initial plan was to participate in the Galloway group once again with the goal of running the Marine Corps Marathon for a time goal. Since some runs with the 10:30 group had proved easy, I asked him if I should begin running with the 9:30 or 10:00 group at the onset of the next season. His answer shocked me. He stated that I should consider staying with my current group or possibly moving to the slower paced 11:00 group. His rationale was that the long runs are not intended to push for time. Their intent is to build endurance. Weekday runs, on the other hand, can be used for speed play to improve race time. Furthermore, he commented that when on increases their pace and has to run harder to maintain that pace, they have a greater potential of getting hurt and thus stunting their overall goals. I understood Ron's thoughts after he provided more rationale behind his answer, but I still had a hard time grasping the idea of potentially running with a slower paced group. I knew that I would have to spend more time thinking about what I felt would be best for me.

At the completion of the course, I was tired, but not completely spent. I was glad to have experienced the hills of Umstead first hand. Yes, there were some tough hills, but my training had prepared me to run through many obstacles. At least tackling the hills is something that is within my control, unlike a nagging injury. I know that running my first marathon will be hard and yes, I probably did not pick the best first marathon course, but I am going to complete the Raleigh City of Oaks marathon on November 1. Completing such a hilly marathon will give me a solid foundation for then running a flatter marathon course with a time goal.

Key points this week:

1. After running more than 20 miles, additional time is needed to allow the body to rest and recuperate. From now on, I will take one full day off from exercise and then do a very low key yoga session or walk on the second day following any run over 20 miles.

2. Daily resting heart rate monitoring is very useful in determining one's fatigue and need for rest. If the resting heart rate is 5 beats above normal, it can be a sign that the person needs additional rest and/or is getting sick.
3. The long runs are utilized to build endurance whereas the shorter weekday runs are used to establish and improve race pace.
4. Umstead Park does have tough hills, but strong runners can run those tough hills. I am tough and strong.

	Monday	Tuesday	Wednesday	Thursday	Friday	Saturday	Sunday
Date	9/14/09	9/15/09	9/16/09	9/17/09	9/18/09	9/19/09	9/20/09
Goal	Run	Swim	Yoga	Run	Rest	Run with group	Rest
Duration	37 min	25 min	42 min	32 min			
Distance	3 miles	?	NA	3.2 miles		10 miles	
AM pulse	---	---	---	---		---	
Weather	Hot, not humid	NA	NA	NA			
Temperature	88°	NA	NA	NA			
Time	12:00 pm	12:10 pm	1:30 pm			?	
Terrain	Slight hills	NA	NA	Treadmill		Hills	
Run/Walk	3:1	NA	NA	Treadmill		3:1	
Rating	6		10	9		8	
Comments	I should have done different exercise instead of running.		Great stretching-very relaxing.	Bored on the treadmill!		I ran Umstead for the first time.	

Table 17-Training Log Week 17

Training Week 18

It would not be a normal week without my typical Monday Durham County 3 mile run. While changing clothes, I realized that I had forgotten my water belt and water bottles. Thus, I opted to run only taking walking breaks if needed. This plan was likely the opposite of what it should have been, but I followed through with it any way. The first mile loop was effortless. It felt really good to be outside and I was very thankful to be running. The second lap took a little more effort, but also felt good. Since I had run the first two laps without breaks, I felt that I also had to run the third lap without walking. Thus, I continued my pace and continued running without walking. Nearing the end of the run, I increased my pace and completed the run at a sprint. I then walked back to the office and did some crunches. Ron had mentioned the previous weekend that increasing core strength can help increase pace. After that conversation, I decided that I would try to start working on my abs as often as possible.

Tuesday was a very hectic day at work. By lunchtime, I needed a mental break. For me, it is very calming to hear the gentle splashing of the water and to feel my body move through the water. I wanted and needed to be calmed. Since the lifeguards were in the process of cleaning a portion of the pool, the swim lanes were more crowded than usual. I paired up with another swimmer and began my quest for inner peace. After getting caught up in the pool vacuum cord during the first and second laps, I debated just getting out of the water and going back to work. Determined to have a few minutes for my sanity, however, I continued swimming. Fortunately, the lifeguard stopped cleaning the pool after a few more laps and I was able to swim unencumbered. As I swam lap after lap, I began to relax more and more. Ultimately, I lost count of my laps and just continued moving back and forth through the water. As I began to break a sweat, I continued to feel the stress of the day easing. I did not care how many laps I swam, I just wanted to swim as long as I could. Ultimately, I swam for a total of 20 minutes without stopping. I then did 4 laps of breast stroke, back stroke and kicking with the kickboard. As I entered the locker room, I felt very content with my workout. I was ready to get back to work and face whatever challenges lay ahead.

If only the contentment obtained on the previous day could have blended over into the next day, I would have had a much better Wednesday. Unfortunately, I again became consumed with work and its stressors. Instead of leaving work at the end of the work day, I stayed late to attempt to complete office notes and calls that were beginning to accumulate. I left work just in time to pick up the kids and then begin the chaos of daily home duties. By the time Bryan got home from work, I had completed many of the tasks for the day, but I had yet to begin making dinner. Wanting to fill my stress coffers with unhealthy foods, I suggested going out to dinner. I wanted a fat, greasy burger and fries. As a health professional, I am supposed to teach people to "Eat to live, not live to eat." That particular day, I was a hypocrite. I felt a little guilty after pigging out at Red Robin since I had let stress consume me and thus dictate my actions. I knew that a better decision would have been to make a change that would have allowed me to reduce my stress and thus get back to more healthy decisions. Thus, once the kids were in bed, I pulled out my work computer and completed all of my office visit notes. My stress level was immediately reduced knowing that I would enter the next work day without unfinished work hanging over my head.

That Thursday, I was determined to complete the day's work while at work. I was also determined to get my workout in for the day. At lunch time, I set out for my typical 3 mile Durham County run. I began running with no water and without taking walking breaks. Soon into the first mile, I was caught off guard by the heat and humidity of the day. I was able to complete the first and second miles without walking, but then opted to take 2 walk breaks on the third and final mile. Ultimately, I completed the run with a descent time of 34 minutes, but realized that I needed to be more cautious with monitoring the weather for change since the fall season had just begun.

Usually Friday is a day reserved to rest for a long Saturday group run, but since I had missed a workout session on Wednesday and I was not sure if I would do my scheduled 10 mile run on either Saturday or Sunday, I opted to head to the gym after work to try out my new cycling shoes. I figured that at least a portion of the workout would be spent manipulating the shoes in and out of the clip. I was at least partially right. I spent a good 5 minutes trying to clip-in for the first time. My problem was obviously clear to others since I attracted the help of 3 trainers into the spinning room to offer their assistance. It seemed that I could get one shoe to clip in, but not the other. Then, I would get the opposite shoe clipped in but only because I had unclipped the other shoe. It was a little frustrating at first, but once I had both feet secured, I was able to cycle with better ease and flow. Spinning is always such a welcomed sweat fest for me and this session was to be no different. Even though I could tell that my endurance was much better than previous, I still had a great workout. It felt great to work out a little aggression with help from singer Katy Perry.

As it turned out, I would tackle my longest run of the week on the following day. Saturday began with a pancake breakfast at Andy's to support the kids' summer swim team. We then ventured to Harrison's soccer game. As we sat on the sideline shivering in the cold, our crazy son kept diving into the ground after the soccer ball. It was like déjà vu given that earlier in the year he often dove after baseballs while playing T-ball on that same field. He had grass up to his neck. When my husband pulled out the camcorder to record a little footage of the game, Harrison stood in the middle of the field posing for the camera. He even pulled a friend into the picture and gave his dad a thumbs-up pose. What a character!

Since I was so cold after sitting outside at the game, I debated just staying home and laying on the cough with a large blanket covering my body. But knowing that I needed to complete a long run this week to prepare for my first 26 mile run the following week, I dragged myself into the bedroom to change into running clothes. I decided to run on the Tobacco Trail close to my home since I knew the course was amenable to a consistently flat 5 mile out and back run. Furthermore, I knew that running the course would be good preparation for running an upcoming race in late October on the same trail.

With my water bottle around my waist, my Gym Boss set for 3:1 intervals and my I-tunes softly playing in my ear, I set out to run alone. I was fortunate to have 2 runners just in front of me to watch throughout most of the first half of the run. Furthermore, the gentle rain provided a continuous coolant on my body. I found it serene to run amidst the tall trees. I took note of the subtle changes of fall beginning to take place. I experienced a religious moment and I thanked God for my surroundings and the ability to run on such a beautiful path. Though I felt strong, I cherished every walk break and paid close attention to my water and electrolyte supplementation. I did experience a brief period of fatigue during the 7th mile, but I recuperated by telling myself that I only had 3 miles left and that 3 miles was my standard weekday run. Once on the final mile, I began to run without walking breaks. I wanted to push myself as fast as I could for the final distance. Ultimately, I completed the run in 1 hour and 52 minutes. I was content with my time and very pleased with the experience. The previous chill of the morning was now far from my thoughts. I was warmed with the sense of accomplishment with yet another strong run.

That evening and the following day, I experienced no stiffness or pain. I had no need for Ibuprofen or prolonged rest. We had family over to celebrate my recent birthday and my husband's upcoming birthday. I splurged on chocolate cake. A friend had once told me that you can eat anything without gaining weight when you are training for a marathon. I wanted to test her theory on that particular day (even though I knew in my head it was false).

Key points this week:

1. Core strengthening can ultimately improve race pace and thus race time.
2. Never get so caught up in your training that you fail to take in the surrounding scenery while running.

	Monday	Tuesday	Wednesday	Thursday	Friday	Saturday	Sunday
Date	9/21/09	9/22/09	9/23/09	9/24/09	9/25/09	9/26/09	9/27/09
Goal	Run	Swim	Too busy for exercise	Run	Bike	Run	Rest
Duration	36 min	35 min		34 min	30 min	1:52	
Distance	3 miles	?		3 miles	?	10 miles	
AM pulse	---	---		---	---	---	
Weather	Cool	NA		Hot & humid	NA	Rainy	
Temperature		NA		88°	NA	?	
Time	12:00 pm	12:00 pm		12:00 pm	12:00 pm	11:00 am	
Terrain	Slight hills	NA		Slight hills	Indoors	Flat	
Run/Walk	3:1	NA		2 walk breaks	NA	3:1	
Rating	9	10		8	8	9	
Comments		Awesome swim!		Caught off guard with humidity	Used new cycling shoes	Ran alone, but felt good.	

Table 18-Training Log Week 18

Training Week 19

Per routine, I started Monday morning with a quick weight prior to taking my shower. I saw the scale briefly hover over 140.5 before settling on 140 pounds. I knew that I felt heavier than usual. I knew that my days of over consuming chocolate cake (and pig pickin' cake earlier the previous week) were over...marathon training or not! I needed to get back into the habit of consuming healthy portions of complex carbs and not excess simple carbs. Unfortunately that evening, my willpower took a vacation yet again and I found myself consuming 3 chocolate coated granola bars for a snack followed by pizza for dinner. Fortunately, I ran my typical Durham County 3 mile loop at lunch and likely burned off about 300 calories. Unfortunately, I knew that I had yet again falling back into the trap of unhealthy snacking.

The next day, I was as usual not eager for exercise. For some reason, Tuesdays are the least motivating days of the week for me. Understanding the importance of regular training, however, I made my way to the gym for a swim. As I entered the water, I felt my mind and body beginning to relax. I started stroking forward and quickly fell easily into my swim strokes. The more I swam, the more relaxed I became. Ten to fifteen minutes into the swim, I felt my body beginning to sweat, but I continued gliding through the pool. I swam effortlessly for a full 25 minutes. Even my flip turns were smooth and uniform. I wished that I could have stayed in the pool to swim to my physical limit, but I needed to get back to work. That swim, however, confirmed that I am becoming a stronger swimmer. Again, the thought of a future triathlon crossed my mind. Another positive experience that day was running into one of the Durham County employees while walking out of the YMCA. As we passed one another in the hallway, Margaret asked me the date of my upcoming marathon. She offered me words of encouragement and stated that I am a great motivator for others. Those words touched me greatly and were truly the icing on the cake after a great workout. Don't worry though, that day I only ate the hypothetical icing on the cake and not the real thing!

Wednesday turned out to be a very hectic day at work. I thus stayed longer to get caught up with my charting. After leaving work, I only had time to get the week's groceries and then pick up the kids. I was able to mow the grass, but there was no time for a true workout. That evening, I attended a beginner triathlon class at a local sporting goods store. Jackie Miller of Britfit Training and Coaching led a very thorough discussion about preparing for your first triathlon. She spent a lot of time talking about methods to better prepare for the swimming and biking segments of the race. She encouraged the use of paddles and fins to improve swimming technique. She encouraged at least 3 if not 4 days of swimming each week. She reviewed the difference between a tri-bike and a street bike, but reassured that even mountain bikes could be up fitted for street riding. She discussed the benefit of bike trainers to allow more flexibility with bike riding. She recommended that everyone have metabolic testing to know their personal lactate threshold or the point at which the athlete shifts from the aerobic metabolic pathway to anaerobic metabolism. Since most of us know our own fitness weaknesses and often avoid working on those weaker areas, she encouraged us all to work with a personal trainer to develop a training program that would help us achieve our racing goals. The whole time that she was talking, I kept contemplating if I was ready to pursue an open water/open road triathlon. Everything that she said intrigued me. I also wondered how much money I would spend attempting to be better equipped for triathlon training. Upon getting home, I bent Bryan's ear for a good hour about EVERYTHING she said. I was then so worked-up that I had a hard time getting to sleep.

I knew that I needed to invest more time into learning about various triathlon distances and venues; however at that particular time, I needed to stop thinking and get some sleep.

Since I was not able to exercise the previous day, I knew that I needed to exercise on Thursday. With the thoughts of a triathlon on my mind, I set out with my ear buds in my ears, a water bottle in hand and my Gym Boss clipped on my shoulder. If I was not physically running with a smile on my face, I was sure running with a smile on my mind. It was an absolutely perfect 70 degree day. It felt absolutely wonderful and I was so grateful for my health and ability to run. I ran the full 3 mile loop with ease. Upon returning from the run, I encountered Bernard and told him about the triathlon class from the previous night. He again told me that he felt that I had great athletic potential. He urged me to pursue further race goals.

The following day, I purposefully consumed a heaping teaspoon full of electrolyte powder in 32 ounces of water to pre-hydrate for the next day's run. I also took a day off from exercise. While the kids were winding down from a day at school, I read through some paperwork for Haley's swim team entitled, "Parents/ Coaches Guides—13 Steps to Being a Winning Parent." Step nine suggested giving your child the gift of failure. "You can't be successful or have peak performances if you are concerned with losing or failing. Teach your child how to view setbacks, mistakes and risk-taking positively and you'll have given him the key to a lifetime of success (www.competitivedge.com/ppg/ppg06.html)." I thought this statement also germane to those setting race goals. Even if one doesn't succeed in achieving his/her full goal, the training improves the person's health and ultimately moves him/ her closer to being able to succeed in the future. Furthermore, failure sweetens the future success. That Friday evening before retiring to bed, I commented to my husband that I looking forward to running my first marathon distance the next day. I honestly was no longer intimidated by running 26 miles. I knew that I could do it and I sensed that I was going to have a good run.

The following morning, I eagerly hopped out of bed, but then realized that I had a splitting estrogen withdrawal headache. Fortunately, I knew that within 30 minutes of taking an 800 mg Ibuprofen, the headache would be significantly reduced. I thus proceeded with getting ready, grabbing my running supplies and hopping in the van. On the way, I consumed my standard breakfast bar and banana with water. I also took my 2 electrolyte capsules and an Ibuprofen. Once at the designated started point for the run, I was gradually greeted by my friendly group members. Even though my headache was starting to subside, the first 2-3 miles were tough as usual. Jeff Galloway states, "The first 15 minutes of every run are a shock to the system. Slow down, get through it and you're on your way (1998, p 58)." As usual, his words reverberated in my head and guided me to much easier running.

The first 10 miles of the run were smooth and easy. I closely monitored both my mileage and time to ensure that I took my electrolyte capsules every hour and my GU supplements every 4 miles. I also made sure to sip either water or electrolyte solution every other walk break. Going into the second 10 miles, I felt strong. At the later miles, Cara tried to conjure up a name game, but this one was more complex that the previous game. I opted to just continue running to ensure that I monitored my pace, arm swing and supplementation. At mile 20, the majority of the group completed their planned distance and left 7 of us to venture out for additional mileage. Missy and Michelle jokingly passed mile 20-21 by talking in French accents. They had us belly laughing while running. At 21.5 miles, 5 runners turned back to complete their needed 23 total miles for the day. This left me and Missy to complete the final 4.5 miles together.

With the aid of Missy's Garmin and good conversation, we pushed forward. I remained diligent with my supplements and hydration. Once at a point when we needed to decided which way to go, we opted to run a slight hill course for a few miles, knowing that we would be turning around and running down the incline towards the finish. We both pushed forward, having meaningful conversation throughout the run. Ultimately, we reached the end of our run, both completing our first 26 mile run. I couldn't believe that I never hit the infamous wall often experienced at about mile 20 of a full marathon. I felt so strong. The tips of my toes were sensitive from over 5 hours of running, but I had no major aches or pains. Upon returning to the parking lot where we started the run, the success of the day was sweetened by Cara giving me and Missy a finisher's medal. What an accomplishment and reward.

On the drive home, I stopped for my typical post run bagel and chocolate milk. Upon getting home and getting out of my van, I noticed stiffness in both of my hips. After a quick shower, I took another 800 mg Ibuprofen and thoroughly stretched out my now aching muscles and joints. Throughout the remainder of the day, I continued feeling stiff after prolonged periods of sitting, but had no truly worrisome pains to spoil the success of the day.

Key points this week:

1. One of my favorite Jeff Galloway quotes is that "The first 15 minutes of every run are a shock to the system. Slow down, get through it and you're on your way (1998, p 58)."
2. It is not uncommon for runners to experience fatigue when only running 3 miles. In order to get to further mileage, one must push themselves beyond the 3 mile mark to realize the ease of running that takes place at longer distances.
3. Paying closer attention to electrolyte and water supplementation throughout a long run will ensure better performance with less injury.
4. Running 26 miles in training prepares one to run 26.2 miles in a full marathon. I am glad that I didn't stop at 23 miles in training.

	Monday	Tuesday	Wednesday	Thursday	Friday	Saturday	Sunday
Date	9/28/09	9/29/09	9/30/09	9/31/09	10/1/09	10/11/09	10/4/09
Goal	Run	Swim	No exercise	Run	Rest	Run with group	Rest
Duration	35 min	25 min		34 min		5 + hours	
Distance	3 miles	?		3 miles		26 miles	
AM pulse	---	---		---		60	64
Weather	Cool with sun	NA					
Temperature	68°	NA		Low 70's			
Time	12:10 pm	12:00 pm		12:10 pm		6:30 am	
Terrain	Slight hills	NA		Slight hills		Flat	
Run/Walk	3:1	NA		3:1		3:1	
Rating	8	10		10		8	
Comments		Wonderful swim!	Triathlon class	Fabulous run!	Hydrate	I did it!	

Table 19-Training Log Week 19

Training Week 20

On the Sunday following my first 26 mile run, I started making a concerted effort to monitor my resting heart rate each morning before getting out of bed. Various Galloway training books discuss the value of monitoring the am pulse rate to determine if one is overtraining (2007, 1998). A level 5% above the norm indicates the need for taking it easy and a rate greater than 10% above the norm suggests the need for a day off from exercise. The morning of my 26 mile run, my resting heart rate was 60. I think that this was slightly higher than average since I awoke anticipating the long run and knowing that I was going to check my pulse. The following morning, my am pulse rate was up to 63. In the mornings to come, I gradually began to see my am pulse rate drop from the 60's to the low 50's. I took this as a sign of recuperation from Saturday's long run.

That Monday, I planned to determine my exercise for the day only after assessing my am heart rate. If it continued to be elevated above 60, my plan was to take it easy and take a walk or do yoga for exercise. I was slightly surprised to count only 56 beats upon awakening. Since my pulse was lower than my pre-23 mile heart rate, I decided to proceed with my typical 3 mile Durham County run at lunch. Similar to my Monday run after the first 23 miler, I noticed a little stiffness in my hips throughout the run; however what was previously an exhausting, never-ending 3 mile run that I rated as a 6/10 for enjoyment was this time a pleasant 8/10 run that I completed in 30 minutes even with taking walk breaks every 3 minutes. It still amazes me at times how the body, my body, can recuperate after long runs.

The following day, my am pulse rate was again in the low 50's; thus I headed to the YMCA for my typical swim during my lunch break. Upon entering the Y, a sign stated that the lap pool was closed for repairs. In my determination to swim, I opted to attempt to swim laps in the general pool area. In order to swim as straight as possible, I purposefully began to swim trying to stay close to the lane divider used to separate the pool walking lane from the play area. Once in the water, I was overcome by the warmth of the water. I wasn't accustomed to swimming in a sauna! As I approached the opposite side of the pool, I realized that I did not have any underwater markers to indicate the end of the pool or when to do a flip turn. I thus stroked forward with my left arm straight into the pool wall. I thought of abandoning my swim but then streamlined my way into a second lap in the pool. I tried to flip turn once without success and thus opted to just touch the wall and streamline into successive laps. While swimming, I thought to myself that during an open water triathlon, there would likely be no underwater lines or indicators to keep me swimming in a straight path. Thus, my current swimming condition was great practice for a future open water swim. With that mindset, I started to relax and stroke more smoothly through the water. My initial thought for the day was to attempt to swim one mile (1760 yards or 70 lengths) in the pool, but I was not able to keep track of the number of laps completed. I did, however, swim continuously for a full 30 minutes. For that, I was proud.

On Wednesday, I had a massage after working until 12:30. I had purposefully scheduled the massage for the week following my first 26 mile run thinking that I would be sore and thus need massage therapy. It even surprised me to utter to the therapist that my 26 mile run had produced no specific areas of concern. I thus asked her to deliver a relaxing, deep tissue massage. As she began her work, however, she quickly found some tender areas. Apparently my rhomboid and trapezius muscles were very tight. The left side was worse than the right. I deduced that the problem stemmed from carrying my computer bag, lunch bag and pocket book daily on my left shoulder. She also isolated some tenderness in the left hip and stated that I could be developing a trigger point on the lateral aspect of the hip at the attachment of the IT band. She recommended more thorough stretching of the hip joint both during and after running. Thoughts of my previous knee pain, deemed IT band pain, briefly entered my mind. Could I be headed for another painful run in the future?

That evening, I felt so great and the fall like weather was so refreshing that I asked Bryan to watch the kids while I went out for an evening run. I had planned on doing yoga, but yearned to be running outdoors. I thus donned my running gear and I-pod to take to the road. As my feet and legs moved me effortlessly down the road, I recollected how that same Olive Chapel run use to be exhausting. I use to yearn for walking breaks and now I was running at a faster pace without walking breaks. After completing the first mile, I decided that I was not going to stop running until I tackled the big hill ahead. As the hill approached, I told myself to stay strong. I purposefully ran in sync with the rhythm of the music playing softly in my ears. I ran that hill strongly and relatively fast. Ultimately, I ran in control of my body and thus did not let the hill control me.

As I descended the hill, I quickly began to prepare for the other steep but shorter hill to come. I knew in my mind that I would not stop until I reached the summit of the second hill. Again, I ran in sync with my music and in total control of my body. That, too, proved to be an easy hill to tackle. I ultimately completed the 4 mile run without any walking breaks and feeling as alive as humanly possible. To date, that is my best and most pleasant run. During that run, I once again experienced the infamous runner's high.

The following day, my am pulse rate remained in the 50's; therefore I knew that my body was tolerating my previous workouts. I decided to go for a spin at the YMCA. During the previous week's triathlon training class, Jackie Miller with BRITFIT stated that a typical cadence for elite triathletes is 85-

95 revolutions per minute (rpm). My goal was to determine my standard cadence and then attempt to keep my pace within the range above. Truthfully, I wanted to know if I could potentially hang with the big guns. I had initially hoped to ride with my I-tunes, but realized after locking into the pedals that my I-pod was at home charging. Knowing that I would likely control my pace and breathing better without listening to music, I started spinning. I measured my standard pace as 82 rpm. I then sped up to about 89 rpm. Every 5 minutes, I counted my cadence and was proud to be consistently between 88-93 rpm. Though music or changing scenery would have helped to pass the time, I enjoyed my 30 minute spin. I was reassured that with the proper training and gear that I would be able to compete against at least the beginner triathletes.

After completing a half day at work that Friday, I took my Columbia trail bike into a local triathlon store to see what it would take to make my bike more road worthy. After the salesman started talking about replacing both wheels and the comfort seat, I knew that upfitting that bike was not an option. I told him that I was contemplating Olympic distance triathlons in the future. He then reviewed the various road bikes and how they differ in weight and gears. I could get the "starter" road bike for about $750.00. He then discussed that a beginning triathlon bike started around $2300.00 and was typically lighter and more aerodynamic than road bikes. I asked why road bikers tend to shun riding with those on tri bikes. He explained that the braking mechanism for a road bike is in the same location as your hands throughout the ride. Thus braking can occur very quickly and reduce the number of bikers from colliding with one another. The braking device on a tri bike is in the same location as a road bike; however, those riding a tri bike often keep their arms and hands on the tri bars and not on the outside bars. Therefore, it may take a few seconds longer to brake appropriately. With inexperienced riders, collisions can be more prevalent. On my way home, I rationalized to myself that it would be somewhat pointless for me to purchase a road bike for $750.00 and then turn around and buy a tri bike for $2300.00 the next year or so. My ultimate goal was not to ride in a pack on the open road, but to compete alone in a triathlon. Now, I just needed to convenience my husband that I needed a tri bike. That would prove difficult.

I wanted to run with the Galloway group that Saturday, especially since they were doing a scavenger run, but I feared that I would be too rushed to get home and get ready to go to a 12:00 Carolina versus Georgia Southern game. I thus decided to go for a 10 mile run by myself. I awoke pretty easily at 6:30 am with a resting heart rate of 54. My initial plan was to run a 10 mile loop from my house onto a local greenway and then on my typical Olive Chapel Road path. I uploaded a time, pace and distance program on my husband's I-phone and set out for the run. Once I completed the greenway path, I pulled out the I-phone to see exactly how many miles I had run and view my average pace. I was so MAD to see that the program had only recorded my running time and not my pace nor distance. Ugh…why carry the extra weight even if it is only a pound or so! I stopped for a moment to reload the program and fortunately it started working as desired. Assuming that I had only ran about 3 miles, I ventured towards a new running path to accumulate mileage.

As I ran, I was not the nervous Nancy that ran circles in Apex in July to accumulate 10 miles. Instead, I was a confident runner using previous long runs to estimate distance while enjoying the novelty of a new running course and scenery. I made up the course along the way, not avoiding hills or new terrain. Towards the end of the run, however, I did find myself in a neighborhood that was unfamiliar. Thus, I had to ask a dog walker where I was and how to get back to the main road. Fortunately, I was in the safety of the Apex area and not far from Olive Chapel Road.

Once at the main road, I began my trek home. Knowing that I likely needed a little more distance to get to the 10 mile mark, I ran a lap around my neighborhood. The I-phone registered 5.25 miles for the second part of the run. I likely only completed an

8-9 mile run, but I was pleased with the run. Upon returning home, I quickly stretched, showered, packed a lunch for tailgating and headed out to my Alma matter. Once in Chapel Hill, Bryan and I realized that we were 3.5 hours early for the game since the start time had been moved from noon to 3:30. To pass the time, we played tag in the quad, saw a one hour science demonstration at the Morehead Planetarium, climbed to the top of the bell tower, watched the kids climb on and through blow-up structures at Tarheel town, and purchased a snack before finally sitting down in our seats to watch Carolina spank Georgia Southern. It was not the day we intended, but wonderful nonetheless.

Key points this week:

1. It is fun to run a new path, but research a little about the area before setting out to run so that you don't get caught in unfamiliar territory.
2. If you are interested in purchasing equipment for participation in triathlons, a starter road bike is approximately $750.00 whereas a tri-bike is approximately $1700.00-$2300.00.
3. Always check the starting time for a collegiate game prior to heading out. If not, you may get burned!

	Monday	Tuesday	Wednesday	Thursday	Friday	Saturday	Sunday
Date	10/5/09	10/6/09	10/7/09	10/8/09	10/9/09	10/10/09	10/11/09
Goal	Run	Swim	Run	Bike	Rest	Run	Rest
Duration	36 min	30 min	60 min	30 min		1:40	
Distance	3 miles	?	4 miles	?		10 miles	
AM pulse	56	---	56	57		54	54
Weather	Great	NA	Great	NA		Cool	
Temperature	75°	NA	65°	NA			
Time	12:10 pm	12:20 pm	6:30 pm	12:15 pm		6:30 am	
Terrain	Slight hills	NA	Slight hills	NA		Slight hills	
Run/Walk	3:1	NA	Run only	NA		4:1	
Rating	8	8	10	9		9	
Comments		Had to swim in regular pool	I ran after a massage and felt great!	Cadence was 85-93 rpm		Good run with a new ratio	

Table 20-Training Log Week 20

Training Week 21

I started the week with my typical Durham County lunch run; however, I opted to run for 4 minutes and walk for 1 minute instead of my usual 3:1 run/walk cycle. My thought was that running for a longer time could allow me to complete the run faster; thus I could gradually begin working on increasing my overall pace and begin running 4 miles during lunch instead of just 3 miles. Once I got outside, I was so pleased with the cool 60 degree temperature that I opted to run through 2 walk breaks. One mile into the run, however, I decided that I really needed the walk breaks and thus began adhering to the 4:1 cycle. After a few walk breaks, I again had the energy to push a little harder while running. On the final lap of the 3 mile loop, I sprinted through one walk break and completed the run. Overall it was not the most satisfying run, but it was nice.

That Tuesday, my plan was to go for a swim at the YMCA, but upon arriving at the gym, I was notified that the pool was still closed for repairs. I had no other work out clothes or shoes and was thus stuck with no means of exercising. I went back to the office for a leisurely lunch and then resumed work. That evening, Bryan got home early from school since his professor was sick with the H_1N_1 virus. I seized the opportunity to have him take the kids to bed while I went into the garage to run on the treadmill. Even though I was watching TV while running, I was bored. I completed 3.5 miles in 30 minutes, but was glad to be done with that workout.

Since it appeared that I would not be able to swim at the Durham County YMCA the whole week, I opted to travel to the Cary YMCA for a swim on Wednesday. Again, my goal was to swim 1 mile (1760 yards or 70 laps) in the pool, but I also wanted to immediately follow the swim with a spin. It was a little odd to change in a different locker room and swim in a different pool, but I kept telling myself that the pool itself was a 25 yard pool just like the one in Durham. Once in the water, there would be no differences. As I began swimming, I felt myself relaxing. The first 250 yards were easy and I felt like all was going well. At 500 yards, I could feel myself sweating, but I intentionally elongated my strokes and paid closer attention to pulling myself through the water. At 750 yards, I thought that swimming another 30 plus lengths of the pool was a crazy and unobtainable goal for the day. Even though, I pushed through 6 more lengths of the pool. I completed 900 of my planned 1760 yards. Upon getting out of the pool, I realized that I had a massive, pounding headache. Previously I had experienced a slight headache after swimming, but nothing like this. While in the lobby transitioning from the pool to the locker room, an older lady said to me, "You swim very well." Boy…she made my day and really boosted my self confidence.

As I changed into my cycling clothes, I thought to myself that I was crazy to be attempting to spin with such a headache. Given my bullheadedness, however, I pushed through the pain, walked outside and around the gym (in the rain) to get to the building with the spin bikes, and mounted a bike. I was perturbed that the spin bike did not have the proper plates for my shoe clips, thus I had to slip my cycling shoes into the stirrups. After about 5 minutes of spinning, my headache subsided. I started feeling a little fatigued 10 minutes into the ride and thus opted to continue spinning for only 5 more minutes. After dismounting the bike, I again traveled out into the rain to the aquatics center to change my clothes. That work out had not been all that I had intended, but I accomplished some of what I planned to do – I swam a meaningful distance and then immediately road a bike. Hum… triathlon on the brain again.

Upon awakening on Thursday, I was a little surprised that my pulse was elevated at 63. I debated not working out at all, but quickly pushed that thought to the back on my mind. Usually on Thursday I would head out for my second run of the week, but I had already had two runs this week; thus, I opted to go to the YMCA for a spin. Unlike last week, I was fully prepared with my spinning shoes and fast tunes to aid in the ride. I mounted the bike, easily clipped in, and began spinning. Within 2 minutes, I was peddling at a rate of 85 rpm. I continued in the saddle at a pace of 85-95 rpm for 35 minutes, but at times unintentionally sped up to 98-99 rpm. It felt wonderful to be peddling so easily and so fast. As usual, the spin was a revitalizing sweat fest! Feeling pushed to get back to work, I only did 5 minutes of abs and stretching prior to proceeding to the locker room to change clothes. I hate that my workouts always seem rushed, but I value that I take the time to do what I can, when I can.

While at the gym on Thursday, the attendant told me that the pool repairs were complete. I thus decided that I would detour from my normal Friday rest day and go to the gym for a swim. My goal would again be to swim a full mile. Throughout my entire work day, I felt tired and sluggish. I seriously debated if it was a sign of physical fatigue or just the blahs from a cold and dreary day. My morning heart rate of 57 was only slightly elevated from the norm and thus not indicative of the need for rest. Feeling compelled to swim and knowing that I had ample time to attempt a long swim, I drove to the Durham County YMCA. My shower to rinse off felt so warm and good that I thought about staying under the shower water, but then I felt silly for thinking about just coming to the gym for just a warm shower. As I got into the water, I was glad that it was warmer than usual, but not the sauna temperature of my previous swim in the general pool. I began stroking and attempting to count every 50 yards in the pool. 1, 2, 3…I counted off the laps. The first 10 laps or 500 yards were easy. During the second 10 laps, I started to sweat. Laps 20-25 were the most difficult, but I kept telling myself that if I made it to 25, I could then count down from 10 to 1 and complete my 35 laps. I pushed through to the 25th lap and, as expected, had a surge of energy knowing that only 10 laps were left. I started purposefully elongating my strokes to move faster through the water. I was amazed at how fast I could swim even though I was more than 30 minutes into my swim. After completing my flip turn towards the end of the 35th lap, I significantly increased my pace. Midway through the final length of the pool, I started cramping in my right foot, but I was determined that nothing was going to stop me now. As I touched the wall and came up for air, I was amazed that I was not gasping for breath. I was tired, but not exhausted. I had completed the full mile swim in approximately 42 minutes. I CAN do ANYTHING that I set my mind to! As I exited the pool, I took note of two other females swimming in the pool. Both had very good form, but one was swimming with a buoy between her legs and swim paddles on each hand. I could not help but wonder what I should now start doing to improve my swim technique.

The following morning, I awoke early to head out for a 10 mile run with the Galloway group. The previous evening, I checked the temperature to see what the weather was going to be like the following day. It was now mid-October and the forecast called for a morning low of 46 and a high of 56. I was a little uncertain of how to dress appropriately for a colder early morning run. I set out a pair of shorts and long pants as well as a tank top and long sleeved shirt. Upon arising, I checked the computer for the most up to date temp. The temperature was 46 as expected. I opted to wear long pants and a tank top covered by a long sleeved pull over. All were of moisture-wicking fabric.

Once at the run site, I was glad that I had opted for the warmest clothes that I had. Everyone was standing around shivering. A co-runner stated that she was not sure if she had dressed appropriately for the run; I shared that I also had the same concerns. Once the run began, I started getting a little warmer. I was sure to keep my hands in the thumb holes of my running shirt to keep my hands covered as much as possible. Once I began to sweat, I contemplated taking off my long sleeved shirt. Boy was I glad that I didn't do that since it soon began to rain. My previously warm body was now again cold. Renee mentioned that she had read that you should dress for 20 degrees above the current temperature to dress appropriately for a run. Ron said that wearing pants is imperative at 30°, but optional at 40°. Gloves were also necessary at 30°, but optional at higher temps. I honestly had never thought about running with gloves. Previously, all of my winter runs took place in a temperature controlled gym. If I were to continue running outside during the winter, I would need to further investigate how to safely run in colder temperatures.

I spent the first half of the 10 mile run taking to Susan about tri-bikes, open water swims, and triathlon events. It was wonderful to bounce a few ideas off of her and get tips from a seasoned triathlete. When it comes to getting information of various race events, there always seems to be someone in our group to ask. About midway through the run, Ron approached me and another runner to ask us if we would be willing to lead a Galloway pace group next year. I was truly honored that he felt that I would be a good leader. I gladly accepted his offer. My hope was to use my experiences to guide others to a successful first half marathon or full marathon.

Upon reaching the 10 mile mark, I was glad that I was not part of the group heading out for additional mileage. I was chilled to the bone and really looking forward to a hot shower. I was surprised that a typical 10 mile run felt different in the cold weather. I had the realization that I no longer needed my sweat towel for wiping away sweat, but for wiping my runny nose. Even though I had learned a lot thus far, I realized that I still had a lot to learn to become an all season runner.

Key points this week:

1. It is not wise to take walk breaks for granted, especially at the beginning of a run. Taking it easy at the beginning ultimately helps you run faster in the end.
2. Pool length conversions for a 25 yard pool:
   1 length = 25 yards
   2 lengths or 1 lap = 50 yards
   4 lengths = 100 yards
   20 lengths = 500 yards = ¼ mile
   32 lengths = 800 yards = ½ mile
   70 lengths = 1760 yards = 1 mile
3. Always check the weather before running and be sure to dress appropriately. A general run of thumb is to wear pants and gloves if it will be 40° or cooler.

	Monday	Tuesday	Wednesday	Thursday	Friday	Saturday	Sunday
Date	10/12/09	10/13/09	10/14/09	10/15/09	10/16/09	10/17/09	10/18/09
Goal	Run	Run	Swim/Bike	Bike	Rest	Run with group	Rest
Duration	36 min	35 min	45 min	30 min			
Distance	3 miles	3.2 miles	900+ yards	?		10 miles	
AM pulse	52	53		63		---	
Weather	Cold	NA	Cold/raining	NA		Cold	
Temperature	60°	NA		NA		46°	
Time	12:00 pm	8:00 pm	1:05 pm	12:05 pm		7:00 am	
Terrain	Slight hills	Treadmill	Indoors	NA		Flat	
Run/Walk	4:1	Treadmill	NA	NA		3:1	
Rating	7	8	8	9		9	
Comments		The pool pump broke; thus I had to change my workout.	30 min swim immediately followed by 15 minutes on bike	Cadence 85-95 rpm			

Table 21-Training Log Week 21

Training Week 22
10 Miler

I started the week with my typical Durham County run, but the cold fall weather made the run seem dramatically different than usual. The temperature was in the upper 40's with a high of only 55o. Again I debated what I should wear. I knew that long pants would be more comfortable, but would I need a long sleeved shirt or short sleeved shirt? I opted for the long pants with a tank top covered by a long sleeved shirt. I figured that I could always remove layers if needed. Not only was my attire a dilemma, but I was a little uneasy about "the reveal" of myself in long running pants. I feel very comfortable with my body and would run in a bikini, weather permitting; however, the employees and constituents of Durham County are not use to seeing me in long running pants. Runners are use to this sight, non-runners are not. I knew that I was going to get looks and possibly comments during this run.

My plan was to run a 4:1 run/walk cycle, but since I left my Gymboss at home, I would have to use my watch as a timer. I ran the first two miles with my long sleeved shirt on. I did not start to sweat until well into the second mile. I definitely felt some staring eyes from the men and glaring eyes from the women as I passed. Some of the men gave me big smiles…I knew what they were thinking! As I started the third mile of the run, I started getting a little warm; thus, I took off my long sleeved shirt to reveal the running tank top that extended to my waist. I was as exposed as I get. After completing the third mile, I realized that it was only 12:34. Thus, I opted to run another mile loop. Midway, I stopped for my last walk break. I then ran a strong pace to complete the four mile run in 36 minutes. Upon the completion of the run, I was glad to get in doors. I couldn't help but wonder what the weather was going to be like the day of my first marathon. Would it be a cold day like today or back to the 70's as is planned for the upcoming weekend? Regardless, I realized that I would at some point soon have a learning curve for adjusting to running in the cold weather.

That Tuesday, I headed to the YMCA for a swim as usual. I swam a mile in 33 minutes and felt great! The following day, I had many errands to run during the day and thus had to run during the evening. I ran my typical Olive Chapel Road route to a greenway behind the Kelly Road Park. As I approached a stopping point on the greenway about 2.5 miles into the run, I noticed that it was starting to get dark. I had hoped to run the full 3 mile greenway and then double back, but opted to turn around for fear of getting caught alone on a slightly secluded trail in the dark. Even with running at a faster pace, dusk approached quicker than my steps and I found myself running in darkness during the last half mile on the greenway. I thus stopped taking walk breaks in hopes of getting to the main road quicker. I continuously looked around, fearing that someone could jump out of the woods at any point. I willed my feet to move faster and my ears to hear any unfamiliar sound.

Upon reaching the end of the greenway and reaching a less secluded area, I finally breathed a sigh of relief. I was also glad to take a walk break. As I began my next run cycle, I made it to the main road. The passing cars were reassuring. I felt my heart rate lowering as my breathing became more relaxed. I started watching my shadow dancing in front of me with each step. Under each lamppost, I evaluated my running strides and body positioning. I looked and felt strong. I thoroughly enjoyed the last mile of the run and felt revived upon completing the run. I vowed to never again get caught in the dark in a secluded area again. If I needed to run in the evening, I would be sure to run in a well lit, well traveled area.

On Thursday, I had lunch with a representative of my company and my new medical assistant and was thus unable to exercise at lunch. I had hoped to do some form of exercise that evening, but there were more important tasks to complete. The following day, I planned to take a break from exercise to prepare for my 10 miler the following day. After work, I took my van in for some general maintenance and ended up waiting 3.5 hours for the work to be completed. The work took so long that I had to ask a neighbor to pick-up my child at the bus stop. Had I chosen to exercise that day, kick boxing would have been a great option. I had a lot of aggression that needed unleashing!

On Saturday, October 24th, I participated in the Tobacco Road 10 Miler in Apex, NC. I chose this race since it was close to my home and on a familiar trail. My training schedule called for a 10 mile run anyway and I figured that running in a race just prior to my first marathon would provide more exposure to race day jitters, but hopefully improved reaction to such stress. One of my fellow Galloway 10:30 group members, Rene, agreed that we would attempt to run the race at a 4:1 run to walk ratio instead of our standard 3:1 cycles. The change was my idea since my hope was to use the 4:1 ratio during the later half of the full marathon the following week.

The race began bright and early on a slightly humid 76° day with rain expected during the morning hours. Almost as soon as the race started, spits of rain began falling from the sky. I really didn't mind the rain, but I was glad when it stopped at about 2 miles into the run. Rene and I ran our typical pace and followed the 4:1 intervals easily for the first half of the run. As we approached the turn around point, we caught our first glimpse of the race leaders. All were running very fast and with a look of pain and passion in their eyes. We were also passed by Cameron, a female woman that lives in my neighborhood. She appeared to be running her planned 8:30 pace. After reaching the midway point, we found ourselves jockeying back and forth with another Galloway group that Rene knew from the 10 minute pace group. Each time they walked, we passed them running. Every time we walked, they resumed the lead. This persisted for about 2 miles until Rene stated that she was starting to tire and thus wanted to slow down to a 3:1 run/walk cycle. She insisted that I continue the 4:1 cycles without her.

At close to the 7th mile, I began running on my own. I continued the 4:1 cycles and the jockeying back and forth with our fellow runners. I thought about just running with them to the end of the race, but then felt that I could push a little harder. During one of the running cycles, I broke away from them and did not see them again until they finished the race. Once alone, I set my eyes on a runner that had been running my pace for miles; however, she was running without walking. I would often catch up to her during the run, but then lose her briefly while walking. Close to the 8th mile, I briefly ran side by side with the female and then passed her. After that, I became determined to not let her pass me.

In the later half of the 8th mile, I was approached by a runner who asked if she could run with me. She stated that she had been watching my run/walk intervals and she wanted to follow suit. She admitted that she had never run 10 miles in training, she was feeling a little tired and she was hoping that using the walking breaks would help her finish the race stronger. As we began running with one another, we passed the next mile with casual conversation. I explained to her how the Galloway method and members had helped me transition from running 3 miles to 26 miles. I told her that my plan was to try to run the last mile without any walk breaks. As the ninth mile approached, however, I opted to continue utilizing the run/walk intervals. I was ready to finish the race, but losing steam. With a half mile to go, we passed a man obviously struggling to finish the race. My new partner encouraged him to join us to the finish. I was so impressed that she thought of another. Joining us did seem to give him more energy and I then fed on his energy. We all became stronger due to her selfless act. Ultimately, the three of us sprinted forward and crossed the finish line at 1:42.48. I averaged a 10.17 mile which I felt was wonderful given that I followed a run/walk cycle throughout the race. I stayed at the finish line to see my former pace girl finish just a minute or so after me. Three minutes later, my friend Rene completed the race. She said that she dropped down to a few 3:1 cycles and then ran without breaks to the finish. She was glad that she had tried 4:1 cycles, but stated that she would likely stick with 3:1 intervals in the future. I felt guilty that I had convinced her to push herself.

Overall, I was pleased with my finish on the 10 mile run. I proved to myself that I could do 4:1 walk/run intervals, but determined that doing so would be tough. I felt as strong physically and mentally as possible for the daunting task that lay ahead for the following week – the first official marathon.

Key points this week:

1. Pay attention to the times for sunrise and sunset to plan your running route safely.
2. Success is sweeter when shared with others.

	Monday	Tuesday	Wednesday	Thursday	Friday	Saturday	Sunday
Date	10/19/09	10/20/09	10/21/09	10/22/09	10/23/09	10/24/09	10/25/09
Goal	Run	Swim	Run	Rest	Rest	Race	Rest
Duration	40 min	33 min	55 min			1:41.48	
Distance	4 miles	1 mile	5 ½ miles			10 miles	
AM pulse	---	---	---			---	
Weather	Cold	NA	Cool			Cool/rain	
Temperature	High 40's	NA	65°			76°	
Time	12:00 pm	12:12 pm	6:15 pm			7:00 am	
Terrain	Slight hills	NA	Flat			Flat	
Run/Walk	4:1, 5:1	NA	4:1			4:1	
Rating	9	10	10			9	
Comments		Felt great!	Ran on a secluded trail in the dark-not smart!			Tobacco Trail 10 Miler	

Table 22-Training Log Week 22

Training Week 23
Full Marathon

My plan for this week was to continue my typical exercise during the earlier part of the week, but take everything at a very relaxed pace to ensure that I did not overstress my body prior to my Sunday marathon. Per usual, I started the week with my normal 3 mile downtown Durham County run, but I used a 4:1 run to walk cycle. It was a cool 65o day and I completed the run in 35 minutes. The following day, I went to the YMCA for my normal Tuesday lunch time swim. I planned to only swim for 30 minutes, regardless of the number of laps swam. I was pleased to complete 42 lengths or 1050 yards, but became a little distressed when I exited the pool and discovered that I had a splitting headache. I think these headaches stem from not breathing as well as needed while swimming.

That Wednesday after work, my plan was to bike the latter half of the City of Oaks full marathon course to familiarize myself with the terrain and elevations. I am the type of person that does not like surprises and thus prefers to plan out everything whenever possible. Inadvertently, however, I missed the turn from Edwards Mill Road to Duraleigh Road and thus ended up riding my trail bike about 3 miles on a very busy and hilly road. Exhausted, frustrated, and pressed for time, I turned around to climb the hill back to my car having never set foot or tire on the race course. Not being able to prepare myself better for the notorious Umstead hills made my slight anxiety worsen. That evening, I had a hard time getting to sleep and started feeling stress induced heartburn. I called my mom (aka my best friend) and vented to her. She allayed my fears and calmed my nerves. I was truly thankful for our girl talk that night.

The following morning at work, I apologized to my new medial assistant for my behavior if I seemed a little snippy or anxious. I explained to her the extent of my 6 months of training for a marathon that was now only days away. She stated that she knew that I had to be a little anxious about what was soon to come. It was nice that sharing my anxiety with her helped the day progress more smoothly. That evening after putting the kids to bed, I decided to do a gentle 30 minute yoga session. I knew that the deep breathing and stretching would help to further reduce my stress and tension. It did as I expected it to do, however I still awoke at 3 am with a somewhat upset and nervous stomach. I was able to return to sleep within the hour, but wished for a full night of uninterrupted sleep.

After work on Friday, I traveled to the McKimmon Center on NC State's campus to work at the Galloway booth for the pre-race health expo. I was truly amazed at how many people came to the booth to share their experiences with the Galloway training program. Many were not officially part of our Raleigh group, but they had read one of Jeff Galloway's books and implemented some form of the run/walk program. One lady told me that her 72 year old father had been running half marathons for years with run/walk breaks progressing as follows: 1:1, 2:1, 3:1, 4:1, 5:1, 6:1, 7:1, 8:1 then 9:1. He would then repeat the process backwards. He knew that as he was getting closer to the second 1:1 ratio, he was getting closer to finishing his run. To me, it seemed a valid, yet confusing running strategy. I met another lady close to my age that was running an 8-8:30 minute per mile pace in half marathons at present, but she wanted to join a group to begin working toward running a full marathon. With each prospective group member, I shared the utility of the Galloway program. I discussed how the program has allowed me to transition from running only 3 miles to now running 26 miles. It was truly an easy sell. I hoped for them the satisfaction and accomplishment that I had gained by being a member of the group.

After returning home from the expo and eating spaghetti for dinner with the family, I checked my emails and received two positive messages. One message was from the coordinators of the Tobacco Trail 10 mile race from the previous week. I had emailed them earlier in the day to see why my race time had failed to be reported in the final race stats. Apparently my chip did register my starting time, but did not record my end time. Fortunately, they would record my chip time as I had measured it on my I-phone at 1:42.43. I knew that recording my time for the event would not be significant to anyone but me, but I was glad to have it as part of history. My second positive email was from a fellow Galloway runner and 10:30 pace group member, Anne. She emailed to see if I would like to meet her on Sunday to run the full marathon together. I was so glad to know that I would not be the only one running the full marathon. I would have someone stimulating with whom to talk. Furthermore, I could push her through her tough times and she could do the same for me. Getting that email was like being able to eat a whole gallon of Breyer's natural vanilla ice cream without gaining any weight! She also agreed to my idea of running 3:1 with the half marathon group to the 8.5 mile mark and then running 4:1 during the latter half of the run. SCORE!

The following day, we met the currently healthy members of the Turner family at a soda shop in Pittsboro for a premature celebration of Haley's 8th birthday. Unfortunately my niece was recuperating from a bought of H_1N_1 and thus her family could not attend the get-together. I ordered a grilled chicken sandwich with chips since it was the healthiest item on the menu. I then gorged myself on Haley's extra large ice cream sundae that she could not humanly consume by herself. As the day progressed, I tried to seize every opportunity to sit down and rest, but attempting to maintain a household and care for 2 young kids left little time for sitting. That evening, Bryan and some other dad's in the neighborhood took the kids trick-or-treating. I lucked out and sat with a neighbor in her driveway to pass out Halloween candy. The plan was to hang-out for a little while with the neighbors after trick-or-treating was complete, but I left the festivities early to get to bed. By 9 o'clock, I had laid out my clothes for the following day, set back all of the clocks by one hour, washed my face and gotten into bed. Fortunately, I fell asleep very easily that night.

I was awakened at 2:30 am by the sound of pouring rain. I began hoping that all of the clouds would empty themselves and thus allow the race to proceed without rain. Upon awakening at 5 am, however, I knew that I was not going to get my wish. It was still raining and the forecast called for 70% showers throughout the day. The temperature was to be 52° with a high of 61°. I spent many minutes debating what to wear. I even checked my running journal to see the exact temperature and comfort level during previous cold runs to assure that I dressed appropriately. Ultimately, I opted to wear my long black running pants with a tank top covered by a long sleeved pullover.

I left home that Sunday morning with ample time to get to the race site, but I was still nervous about getting parked and to the predetermined meeting spot. As I got out of my car, I was very surprised when another runner approached me to ask me what I thought she should wear. She stated that this was her first marathon and she was not sure if she should wear her 100% cotton long sleeved shirt or her new commemorative long sleeved race shirt. I told her that it is always better to avoid wearing new clothes on race day, but that her new technical shirt would be better at wicking water away from her body. Little did she know that I was new to all this as well and that I had the same dilemma over what to wear earlier in the morning. I guess I just looked like I knew what I was doing.

As I walked to the staging area, I was so glad to quickly find other members of the Galloway group. I was most pleased to see Anne given that only she and I would be running the full 26.2 miles together. As we stood there in the rain, we all shivered and discussed how cold this run was going to be. Fifteen minutes later, we were all very glad to move to the starting line. Soon after, I was surprised when the mass in front of me started to move. There were no announcements, welcoming words or anthems. There was not even an audible siren or whistle. We just started the race without any pomp or circumstance. Later, I realized that the use of audio equipment was likely abandoned due to the rain. Regardless, I was glad to get moving.

Throughout the initial stages of the run, I gave everyone the turn by turn since I had committed the bulk of the race course to memory. I even knew when to anticipate every hill. As we began to approach downtown Raleigh, the rain began to pour and the wind started to blow very hard. Many hats flew into the air. Others were running while holding their hats on their heads. This was not what I had signed-up for! Even with the terrible weather, we all pushed forward. I announced the upcoming hill on Clark Street. We were all pleasantly surprised when a walk break came right at the peak of the incline. We passed the first few miles with chit chat and all became a little warmer with movement and the distraction of one another's company. Around mile 7, we passed Ron, our Galloway leader. It was great to see a familiar face and receive his positive praise.

As we approached the 8.5 mile mark, we said our goodbyes to those Galloway members running the half marathon. Anne and I then began our trek alone. A constant stream of rain continued falling upon us. We were both feeling good and running strong; however, I spoke up that I would prefer to maintain the 3:1 walk/run ratio instead of changing to a 4:1 cycle as previously planned. I wanted to prevent running poorly at the end of the marathon. Anne graciously agreed.

As we continued to run, all that we could both think about was getting to and getting through the Umstead portion of the run. We both feared the hills, but knew that we would be mentally stronger once that portion of the run was behind us. The number of runners around us was significantly less than previous and everyone seemed to be slowing down. Anne and I, however, seemed to be keeping with our 10 minute mile pace. Our run on Ebenezer Church Road seemed to last forever; thus upon reaching the 12 mile mark, I needed a little pick-me-up. I suggested that we turn on our I-Pods and lose ourselves in some music. Ann, too, thought this to be a good idea. My first song was One Republic's "Say (All I need)." The phrase of the song "all I need, is the air I breathe..." filled me with a much needed positive vibe. The following lyric, "and a place to rest my head," made me chuckle. It would have been real nice to snuggle down into a warm, dry bed to rest my head. I, however, still had work to do. The next song by the Black Eyed Peas, "Boom Boom Pow" really got me going. I found a new pep to my step as I ran and sang the chorus to the song. When we crossed the 13.1 mile mark at 2:24.23, I knew that I was half way to completing my first marathon. I was also reassured that I was still on pace to finish the race in under 5 hours. My optimistic goal was to finish in less than 4:45. My lofty aspiration was to have a great negative split (when the second half of the race is ran faster than the first half of the race) and finish at 4:30. This potential filled me with much needed energy.

Both Anne and I were elated to reach the Umstead path at our 15th mile. We found that the path's once sandy, fine gravel had been reduced to craters of mud puddles. A few runners in front of us were purposefully jumping into the puddles and saturating themselves with mud. I purposefully avoided the big puddles, but found it amusing to be running through the mud in the rain. I was very glad to have on long running pants to prevent some of the mess from accumulating on my lower legs.

As we continued running, I was happy to see the familiar "graveyard" on my left. I finally knew where I was on the Umstead path! Furthermore, I was elated to realize that we were going to run down the largest hill in Umstead and then climb a smaller hill just prior to exiting the trail. This realization gave me a little extra boost. Within minutes, however, my bubble was burst when Anne started cramping. Anne encouraged me to run ahead of her, but I so wanted the two of us to finish together. I gave her an electrolyte capsule, but it was a little too late. At the end of the next walk cycle, I was ready to begin running, but Anne needed to continue walking. We walked through one full run cycle together, but at mile 16.5, I chose to venture forward on my own. I was feeling great at the time and knew that I could finish stronger on my own.

Once alone, I knew that I would stick to the 3:1 run to walk ratio throughout the race. But, as I approached a down hill portion of the path, I opted to run through a walk break. I wanted to make up some time for walking through a full run cycle. On the other side of the decline was a significant uphill climb. I found myself fatiguing mentally. I felt the full weight of the notorious, never-ending Umstead hill. I regretted running through my last walk break. Now both mentally and physically fatigued, I intentionally stopped running prior to my next scheduled walk break. I told myself that I would resume running at the crest of the hill. I did as planned, but felt that some of the wind had been taken out of my sails. I so wanted to follow the 3:1 run/walk cycles habitually. I knew that relying on my Gym Boss to guide me to the finish would be my saving grace. Furthermore, I knew that I would feel tired at the end of each run cycle, but then regain strength by the end of the walk. That had been my experience in the past and I needed to rely on that experience now.

Upon exiting Umstead, I was elated to be forging on towards the finish line, yet I was dismayed that I was still 7 miles from completing the race. I was also at the exact location where I had previously started cramping during week 10 of training on my first 16 mile run. As soon as that realization came to mind, the mental energy that I had began to wane. I was planning to call my husband at mile marker 20 to let him know to leave our home and begin his journey with the kids to the finish line to pick me up, but hoping that hearing his voice would give me some strength, I opted to call him a little early. It took minutes to move my numb, stiff fingers over the keys of the phone. I incorrectly dialed our familiar number at least twice. Once I had him on the line, I expressed to him that I was miserably cold and longing to finish the marathon. He said, "You can do it baby!" Upon hearing his words, I knew that I had to keep pushing forward. For a few minutes, I debated looking at the phone to see my current race time. My initial thought was that looking at the time would help me push harder to the finish. As I continued to fumble over the keys to the I-phone, however, I opted to just put the phone away and concentrate on running. At that point, I honestly did not care what my race time was adding up to be. I just wanted to finish the race!

After the 20th mile, I started walking up every hill regardless of what my Gym Boss was indicating. I could not run another hill. I felt that running another hill would not only reduce my ability to finish the race, but would also break my spirit. Knowing that I was now walking a lot more than intended was already breaking my spirit. I was hitting "the wall" and feeling depleted with every step. I was wet. I was cold. My right hip was starting to hurt. My legs felt like lead. I was miserable!

As I approached the water stop at mile marker 22, I truly was in a state of self doubt. As if straight from God, I looked up and saw the familiar faces of Ron and Eric, 2 of the Galloway leaders. I screamed their name with a broken voice that barely resembled my own. I held out both arms as if to embrace them both. Tears began streaming from my eyes. I heard Ron say, "Stephanie you can do this." I then saw another familiar face passing out water. As my eyes met Cara's, I began to sob. She knew my soul. I heard her shout, "I love you girl." I tried to will my fingers into the "I love you" hand gesture, but it took so much energy to move my fingers and hold them into the air that I just had to settle with the reciprocal thought in my mind. Seeing the Galloway group brought me back to the reality that I had run 26 miles in the past; thus I could do it again. I had conquered cramping, fatigue and rain in the past; thus I could do it again. I use to run no more than 3 miles and now I was only a little over 4 miles from completing my first official marathon. I just had to think of this as running the Durham County loop 4 times.

My mindset shifted and I was back in the race. I was going to follow the cues from my Gym Boss and be consistent with the 3:1 run/walk intervals. I would run the hills, because damn it, I had done it before. I was not only going to finish this race, but I was going to do it on my terms. For the next 3 miles, I did exactly what I had set my mind to do. I realized that I was now passing many of the individuals that I had seen running throughout the entire race. I approached and passed a very physically fit African American man carrying an American flag. I told myself that if he could run this whole race carrying that flag, then I could surely do it without the extra weight. As I ran down Hillsborough Street, I noticed another man in front of me suffering from an obvious cramp in his right leg. He was pulling his straightened leg forward with each step. I, too, was suffering from a cramp at that time, but my cramp paled in comparison to his. Upon each transition from running to walking, a serge of fire traveled into my right hip. The pain would subside while I was walking, but resume with running. It then took a solid 30 seconds of running to get the pain to once again resolve. I feared that my cramping would ultimately prohibit me from running, but seeing the limping man in front of me compelled me to at least try to continue running. I was not at the degree of pain that he was experiencing and I only had 1.5 miles to go.

As I turned right onto Pullen Road, I knew that I was not far from the finish line. I passed a spectator ringing a cow bell who told me I only had 1 kilometer to go. I had no intellectual capacity at that time to convert kilometers to miles, thus I had no real understanding of what distance remained. Thus, I kept running and made another right hand turn. At the end of Western Boulevard was a steep hill. I opted to walk the hill to preserve my energy. I then continued to walk during a walk break. When the Gym Boss prompted me to begin running, I really did not want to run. The road was at a very slight incline, but even that seemed insurmountable at that point. I told myself that I could rest later. The more I ran, the sooner it would all be over. Though my pace was slower than previous, I ran.

As I turned left onto Nazareth Street, I knew that I only had two right turns remaining before reaching the finish line. I told myself to keep running. I began hearing cheers in the distance and knew that soon those cheers were going to be for me. I told myself, "Keep pushing Stephanie. You can do it. You are about to finish your first marathon. Finish strong...this is for your soul!" As I made the last right turn, I began to unfold the banner that had been hanging on my water belt the entire race. I unraveled the banner just in time for the photographer to snap a few pictures. I began yelling, "It is my daughter's 8th birthday." I then looked to the right of the course to see my family. Haley blushed when she saw my banner that said, "Happy 8th Birthday Haley." I encouraged her and Harrison to come onto the course with me to finish the race. Harrison ran quickly ahead while Haley stopped twice to replace the flip-flops that kept falling off her feet. She finally held the shoes in her hand and we all three crossed the finish line together at 4:54.37. I did it…I completed my first marathon! Even in the cold, wind and rain, I finished in less than 5 hours. I donned my much earned City of Oaks medal, wrapped up in a Dunkin Donut race blanket, kissed my kids, and walked off the race course. I then fell into my husband's arms and began sobbing. I was so grateful to have him with me. I was so glad to have just finished such a grueling event. My tears were both tears of joy and tears of physical pain. I ran a marathon!

Within minutes, I was jolted back to reality by both kids requesting lunch. I told them that I had to stretch first, but we would then get something to eat. Stretching hurt so good but was a true necessity. With heavy legs and a chill to the bone, I then began to hobble/walk to the van with my family. It felt so good to sit down on the van seat. We left the race site hoping to find a nearby restaurant serving pizza, but soon realized that the pizza shop that we had chosen did not have indoor seating. Therefore, we opted to dine in at a burger joint. At that point, I did not care what I ate, as long as I could sit down and get away from the elements outdoors.

After ordering, I slipped into the bathroom to change out of my saturated race clothes. My fingers were so numb that it took at least 15 minutes to peel off my wet clothes and put on dry clothes. As I walked back to my table, I felt sympathy in the eyes of those I passed. They knew what I had just done and could sense my agony. Once we got our food, I was surprised that I was not famished. Instead, I ate my cheese burger with only a small number of fries. I had a slightly uneasy stomach that I contributed to the 5 GU supplements that I had consumed throughout the marathon.

Upon getting home, I took a very long, hot shower. I figured that the race itself was cold enough to count as my post race ice bath. I then took both Haley and Harrison to Harrison's friend's birthday party. Haley later expressed dislike that she had to attend a marathon and someone else's birthday party on her own birthday, but I reassured her that she would forgive me on the following weekend when she and two friends walked into the American Girl store in Alpharetta, Georgia to officially celebrate her birthday. While at the party, I consumed 2 pieces of cheese pizza and my queasiness finally subsided. I found it hard to remain seated due to cramping, but felt riddled with stiffness with each transition to movement.

The stiffness only increased the following day. Unfortunately, I did not take the day off and thus I had to work a full schedule. I am never one to take the elevator, but climbing stairs was difficult that particular day. Conversely, descending stairs was treacherous. I found it somewhat amusing that I ran 26.2 miles the previous day, but could barely walk the following day. I wondered if and when the aching in my left lateral thigh and knee would improve. I wondered when my body would feel normal again. Lastly, I wondered if I would ever want to run another marathon.

Key points this week:

1. A negative split is when the second half of the race is ran faster than the first half of the race. Many feel that striving for and accomplishing a negative split shows good preservation of energy in the earlier stages of the race that allows for improved speed in the later half of the race.
2. It really helps to see a familiar face in the later stages of a race. If possible, plant that familiar face where you feel you need it most.
3. It does help to run your goal distance in training so that when you hit "the wall" during your race, you can draw on previous experience to push through to the finish.
4. Don't plan to work the day after running a marathon. Ideally, keep your schedule flexible to allow for added rest and reduced mobility if needed.
5. Plan a rewarding massage as soon as possible following your race. It is an indulgence that is worthwhile financially, physically and mentally.

	Monday	Tuesday	Wednesday	Thursday	Friday	Saturday	Sunday
Date	10/26/09	10/27/09	10/28/09	10/29/09	10/30/09	10/31/09	11/1/09
Goal	Run	Swim	Bike	Yoga	Rest	Rest	Race
Duration	35 min	30 min	20 min				4:54.37
Distance	3 miles	1050 yards	?				26.2 miles
AM pulse	65	---	---				---
Weather	Cool	NA	Cool				Cold, raining, windy
Temperature	65°	NA					52°
Time	12:10 pm	12:10 pm	1:30 pm				7:00 am
Terrain	Slight hills	NA	Hills				Hills
Run/Walk	4:1	NA	NA				3:1
Rating	9	8	3				7
Comments		Killer headache after the swim	Did not make it onto the right course-very frustrating!		Volunteered at the expo	Halloween	Tough-but I did it!

Table 23-Training Log Week 23

SOUL

Future Plans

The two days following the marathon were definitely the hardest. Every movement took effort. I found it hard to believe that I ran 26.2 miles. I wondered if and when I would be able to move without pain. Never before, even in training, had I been so cognoscente of every movement. I questioned if I should refrain from exercise or attempt some form of stretching or walking to work off some of the lactic acid that had accumulated within my muscles. I didn't want to over-do-it, but I felt that I needed to do something. Two days after running the marathon, I opted to go for a swim. I thought that the water would be forgiving to my aching joints. Even though I did not have a very good swim, it did reduce a lot of the joint stiffness that I was experiencing. Three days after the marathon, I followed through with a previously scheduled massage. I thought that the swimming had alleviated a lot of my aching, but boy was I wrong! I was amazed at how many sore spots my masseuse identified on my hips and quadriceps. Usually I am able to tolerate a pretty deep tissue massage, but I found myself retracting from her touch. My left side had cramped during the race, but my right side was apparently a mess as well. I suspect that the right side had become problematic from compensating for the left side. Even though the massage was more painful than expected, I felt more mobile upon getting up from the massage table. I felt that my joints were again lubricated and able to move more freely. The following day, I was impressed that I was finally able to walk and take the stairs without pain.

I ran for the first time 4 days after the marathon. I was sure to run at a slower pace and take every walk break at the completion of a 3 minute run. I experienced very little stiffness while running and felt exceptional after stretching. I took the next 2 days off to travel to Atlanta to celebrate Haley's 8th birthday. She was so tickled to experience that American Girl store first hand. I am sure that her woes of attending my marathon and her brother's friend's party on her actual birthday were far from her mind.

The following day, I felt compelled to go for a long run since I was again going to be traveling in the van for a prolonged period of time. My initial thought was to run 10 miles, but half way into the run, I opted to head home early. I felt more tired than usual and did not want to over-exert myself. I completed approximately 6 miles without significant aches and pains.

During the next week at work, I resumed my typical workout routine of running the Durham County loop on Monday, swimming on Tuesday, and Yoga on Wednesday. Due to rain on Thursday, I opted to ride the bike at the YMCA. That Saturday, I ran 10 miles with the Galloway group and announced that I had registered for the inaugural Tobacco Road Marathon on March 21, 2010 in Cary, North Carolina. Even though my first marathon was a grueling experience, I did it. I set a goal for myself, trained for 6 months, and accomplished the completion of my first marathon. Now my goal was to not only complete my next marathon, but work on improving my time. My initial thought was to work towards running 4:1 intervals instead of 3:1 intervals and begin incorporating some speed work into my weekday training. I would love to complete the next marathon in less time than what it took for Oprah to run her first marathon, 4:30. Why beat Oprah…well why not! As I begin my training, I will further evaluate if that goal is truly realistic.

Another race that I plan to run in 2010 is the USMC Mud Run in Columbia, South Carolina. That run entails climbing walls, jumping through tires, crawling under a rope course, and carrying a team-member across the finish line. That event would definitely add a little variety to my race schedule. Lastly, I also hope to run the 35th Marine Corps Marathon on October 31, 2010. If I fail to achieve my 4:30 race time in the Tobacco Road marathon, I will likely set the same goal for the later marathon. This would be especially symbolic since that was the marathon in which Oprah ran her 4:30 time. Again I think...if she can do it, I can do it!

Many times throughout the last 6 months, I debated getting involved with triathlons in 2010. My thought was to progress away from running marathon distances and transition into the Olympic distance triathlons. After reviewing numerous sample training schedules for Olympic distance triathlons, however, I have decided that I do not currently have the time to devote to completing further marathons and getting in long bike rides to develop the stamina for Olympic distances. Plus, I feel the need to progress a little further in my marathon training and pace to develop a sense of pushing myself to the best of my abilities. I don't foresee that I will continue running marathons for years, but I will attempt at least 2 more. Furthermore, I feel that it would truly be a sense of accomplishment and pride to complete on of the most notorious marathons, the Marine Corps Marathon. Maybe if time and energy allow, I will slip in a few sprint distance triathlons to get a better feel for participating in triathlons, swimming in open water and navigating transitions. I will definitely repeat my indoor triathlon at Lifetime Fitness in March of 2010 to see how my fitness level has progressed as compared to the previous year. Any other events are yet to be determined.

In addition to the race goals I have set for next year, my upmost goal is to remain healthy and active. I will continue to find time to take care of myself both physically and mentally. I will follow the recommendations of Christiane Northrup and find time for myself. My health is a gift that I plan to nurture for the rest of my life. Then, I will be able to continue to provide loving care to my family and friends.

Key points this week:

1. Give ample time prior to setting your next race goal; however, you may be surprised at how soon you commit to your next race goals.

Take Home Message

I have learned so much about myself during the last 6 months while training to run my first marathon. I have confirmed that I am very goal oriented and that having such goals keeps me motivated to push myself harder. I have become both mentally and physically strong. I now know that running the first 10 minutes and last 10 minutes of any run is the hardest, but that the minutes within those times can be both long and enjoyable. Getting going is truly the hardest part.

I have found a new respect for the benefit of running with a group and the value of utilizing the Galloway running method. I have become a leader when I was previously a follower. I have made new friendships that will last a lifetime. I have confirmed that I have the support of previous friends as well as family to encourage me towards any aspiration. I will continue setting high goals for myself, but hope that others will join me to enrich the journey.

Many of the significant events in my life can be linked to specific dates and times. For example, I was married at 12 noon on August 17th, 1996. Haley was born at 12:52 am on November 1, 2001. Harrison was born 3 years later at 8:24 pm on December 31. This year, I have added to more significant dates and times in my life. I ran my first half marathon on September 6, 2009 in 2:17.10. I then completed my first full marathon on November 1, 2009 in 4:54.37. I wonder what times I will add next year. Will I attain a PR (personal record) in my second or third marathon? Will I ever graduate from a "slow marathoner" and break the 4 hour marathon time? One thing I know for sure is that running lends itself to setting and achieving numerous goals. Personally,

I have finally found a sport that truly captures the essence of my being and will keep me strong both mentally and physically throughout my years. I look forward to the journey of which my goals will lead.

RESOURCES

Jeff Galloway Training Programs
Training programs are available in many states.
http://www.jeffgalloway.com/training/index.html

Spark People
http://www.sparkpeople.com

References

Clark, N. 2008. *Nancy Clark's Sports Nutrition Guidebook* 4th ed. Massachusetts: Human Kinetics.

Galloway, J. 1998. *Jeff Galloway's Training Journal.* Georgia: Phidippides Publications.

Martin, C. 2008. Take Care of Yourself. [Online]. Experience Life. Available: www.experiencelifemag.com/issues/january-february-2008/health-wellness/take-care-of-yourself.html.

APPENDIX A– SPARKPEOPLE.COM DIETARY INTAKE

Appendix A– Sparkpeople.com Dietary Intake

SATURDAY, JULY 18, 2009

BREAKFAST

	Calories	Fat	Carbohydrates	Protein	Sodium, Na
Nutra Grain Bar (Strawberry), 1 serving	130	3	24	2	120
Banana, fresh, 1 medium (7" to 7-7/8" long)	109	1	28	1	1
MEAL TOTALS:	**239**	**4**	**52**	**3**	**121**

LUNCH

	Calories	Fat	Carbohydrates	Protein	Sodium, Na
Lean Cuisine Tortilla Crusted Fish, 1 serving	330	9	45	16	540
Vegetables, Mixed Salad Greens, 1 serving(s)	15	0	3	1	10
Carrots, raw, 1 strip, medium	2	0	0	0	3
Tomatoes, red, ripe, raw, year round average, 0.5 cup cherry tomatoes	16	0	3	1	7
MEAL TOTALS:	**362**	**9**	**52**	**18**	**559**

DINNER

	Calories	Fat	Carbohydrates	Protein	Sodium, Na
Firebird's Sesame Salmon, 202 gram(s)	685	61	10	26	454
Spinach, fresh, 1 cup	7	0	1	1	24
Mashed Potatoes, 1 cup	162	1	37	4	636
White Wine, 1 fl oz	20	0	0	0	1
White Bread, 1 slice, large	80	1	15	2	204
MEAL TOTALS:	**953**	**63**	**63**	**33**	**1,320**

SNACK

	Calories	Fat	Carbohydrates	Protein	Sodium, Na
Diet Coke, 12 oz	0	0	0	0	40
Panera Chocolate Chip Bagel, 1 serving	370	6	69	10	480
Yoplait Mixed Berry, Yogurt, 1 serving	170	2	33	5	80
Panera Bread Plain Low Fat Cream Cheese, 2 tbsp	130	0	0	0	0
Cake, chocolate, with chocolate frosting, 1 piece (1/8 of 18 oz cake)	235	10	35	3	214
Trader Joe's Veggie Sticks - 50 sticks, 0.5 serving	70	4	9	1	150
MEAL TOTALS:	**975**	**22**	**146**	**18**	**964**

RUNNING SUPPLEMENTS

	Calories	Fat	Carbohydrates	Protein	Sodium, Na
Gu Energy Gel, 1 serving	100	0	25	0	40
Fig Newton, Fat Free (2 cookies), 2 servings	180	0	44	2	260
Cliff Shot Blocks (strawberry, 0.33 servings	33	0	8	0	23
MEAL TOTALS:	**313**	**0**	**77**	**2**	**323**
DAILY TOTALS:	**2,842**	**98**	**390**	**74**	**3,287**
DAILY GOAL:	1755 - 2485	48 - 78	417 - 695	60 - 158	500 - 2300

Appendix B–Sparkpeople.com Weekly Cardio

Appendix B-Sparkpeople.com Weekly Cardio

Printable Weekly Cardio

PRINT THIS

PREVIOUS WEEK

NEXT WEEK

CARDIOVASCULAR EXERCISE FOR THE WEEK OF 7/12/2009 - 7/18/2009

	EXERCISE	MINUTES	CALORIES BURNED
Sunday:			
Monday:	Running: 11 min/mile (jogging)	33	293
Tuesday:	Swimming: crawl	30	325
Wednesday:	Yoga	45	116
Thursday:	Running: 10 min/mile (jogging)	30	296
Friday:			
Saturday:	Running: 12 min/mile (jogging)	180	1418
	WEEKLY TOTALS:	**318**	**2448**
	WEEKLY GOAL:		760

About the Author

Stephanie Turner is a full-time certified Family Nurse Practitioner. During six months of training using the Galloway run/walk method, she was able to successfully complete her first half marathon, 10-miler, and full marathon. Turner and her husband have two children and live in Apex, North Carolina.